Flamingo's

Baby

David Medansky

Second Edition
2015
MMXV

All of the characters and events in this book are fictitious, and any resemblance to actual persons, living or dead, is purely coincidental. Except for obvious historical events, this book is entirely a work of the imagination. There is no Valentina Benjamin. To the best of the author's knowledge and information Benjamin Siegel and Virginia Hill did not have any children named Valentina. This is a work of fiction. Names, characters, places, and incidents either are the product of the authors' imaginations or are used fictitiously. Any resemblance to actual events, locales, organizations, or persons, living or dead, is entirely coincidental and beyond the intent of either the author or the publisher.

Library of Congress Control Number: 2014922250

Copyright Registration Number: TXu 1-913-574
(Dream Town – Heart of Vegas)

Medansky, David Flamingo's Baby
I. Title 1. Las Vegas. 2. Gangster. 3. Gaming

ISBN-13: 978-1511720977
ISBN-10: 1511720972

CreateSpace Independent Publishing Platform
North Charleston, South Carolina

10 9 8 7 6 5 4 3 2

ACKNOWLEDGMENTS

This novel is dedicated to my parents Lloyd and Eileen and to my wife, Debbie.

This novel is also dedicated in loving memory to:

Lawrence Allen Medansky

April 7, 1955 – July 14, 1974

"Some people come into your life for a reason. Others come for a season."

Special thanks to Russell Seale for creating the idea of Flamingo's Baby (Originally entitled "Dream Town"). Without Russell's creative genius, this novel never would have been started.

Special thanks to Corinne Mercier for making this a better story with her editing and proofreading of this novel.

Editing: Will Duffy, Corinne Mercier, Nikiana Medansky
Proofreading by: Corinne Mercier, Bette Small, Nikiana Medansky
Author's photo taken by: Nikiana Medansky

Prologue:

Truth is always malleable.

June 18, 1947: Beverly Hills, California.

Her mood was somber. His was one of despair. Despite the hostility towards each other – each knew deep down that the other was right. The living room of Virginia's Beverly Hills home dimly lit by a single light evidenced the elegance which once belonged to Rudolph Valentino. Virginia was renting the mansion where Ben had retired after the disastrous opening of the "Dirty Bird" around Christmas, 1946. The Dirty Bird was also known as the Flamingo Hotel and Casino, in Las Vegas. Virginia was having another heated discussion with the greatest love of her life, Benjamin Siegel.

Virginia, otherwise affectionately known as "The Flamingo," a nickname given to her by Siegel because of her long legs, occasionally traveled to Mexico City with her brother Chick. She would drink staggering quantities of liquor and was seen in the gambling halls very often with her red hair framing her flushed face. Another story has it that the Mexican casino men gave her the nickname "The Flamingo." Either way, it was a name that stuck.

Ben was not happy about the information Virginia had just told him. She had hidden two million dollars of Meyer Lansky's money that was meant to be used for the Flamingo; money she had stolen outright. Then, as an afterthought, she informed Ben that she had placed their four month old daughter, Valentina, up for adoption with a couple she'd just recently met.

"How could you do such a stupid thing," he shouted. "I told

you . . ."

He was cut-off in mid sentence as Virginia, wearing a bright knee length green summer dress, her face turning a bright shade of ruby red flustered with anger, screamed back, "You made it perfectly clear - she was my problem."

Ben, dressed in a Chadwick gray v-neck wool sweater vest, a white dress shirt and black slacks, the veins in his neck bulging out, yelled back, "Yeah but I didn't know--"

Virginia didn't let Ben finish his sentence as she interrupted, "You didn't know someone could be more important to you than your damn casino?"

In a much calmer voice, Ben said, "It takes a lot of work to make a dream come true, sweetie. . ."

Virginia also calming down, her face returning to its normal pale white shade of color, said, "Ben, the dream is over."

Ben countered, "No, it's only just begun. You'll see. Everyone will know I am a true visionary. Las Vegas will be the entertainment Mecca of the world."

Virginia threw open the front door of the house, exiting in a huff. She got into her red 1947 convertible Bentley leaving Ben alone. He stared out the window stunned by what had just happened, wondering what had become of his life. The Flamingo was a bust. His investors and business partners, Meyer Lansky and Jake Stacher, wanted to know where the missing money, an extra $2 million in cash, had been stashed. Now that Virginia informed Ben that she had hidden the money in various places to keep it "safe," he could no longer honestly defend her. He lied, however, and told his partners he didn't know what happened to the money.

Ben had earlier been informed by his close associate, Mickey Cohen, that Virginia held a secret Swiss bank account. Ben, blinded by love, refused to hear anything negative about her. He trusted her implicitly. To Ben, money was just dirty pieces of paper with ink printed on it. He could always get more.

Early the next morning, Virginia left Beverly Hills for Paris on Pan American flight 868. Virginia had a premonition that something ominous was coming. She was one smart and savvy woman. She was not going to be a part of what she thought was coming. As the metallic silvery, plane ascended into the majestic sky, Virginia took one last look at Los Angeles not knowing what was to become of her and Ben.

*　*　*

Two days later, on June 20, 1947, at approximately 10:00 p.m., Ben and Al Smiley were sitting side by side on the floral couch in Virginia's living room. Ben was wearing a grey suit, white shirt with cuff links and a wide blue tie. On his left hand he wore a gold pinky ring with a large "S" engraved on the surface. The *Los Angeles Times* was spread open across Ben's lap. Ben was reading an article about the death of Elizabeth Short also known as the Black Dahlia. On January 15, 1947, Short's brutally mutilated body was found in the Leimert Park district of Los Angles, California, by Betty Bersinger and her three year old daughter. Short's gruesome murder was all over the news and much-publicized at the time.

The room he sat in was not attractive, despite Virginia's

expensive decorating. An oil painting of an English dowager hung on one wall beside the fireplace. Among the Moroccan touches was a small bronze statue of Cupid next to fireplace tongs and a poker. Ben had the curtains slightly drawn. The valances were the same floral print as the couch. The floral sofa seemed out of place in the Moorish-style setting. In front of the floral couch was a French provincial marble coffee table. On it was an ashtray, a small decorative box and bronze art deco statue of a woman holding her hands above her head as if receiving manna from heaven.

There was a man outside the window of the room standing behind the lattice frame. He had a clear view of Ben through the partially drawn drapes. Ben, engrossed in his conversation with Al, did not see him. A .30-06 carbine was resting in a notch of the lattice. Lined up in the gunman's sights was Ben's handsome face.

Suddenly, without warning, a series of loud noises, like firecrackers exploding, rang out. Before Ben could react, shots were being fired that shattered the picture window of the living room.

At approximately 10:30 p.m., on Jack Dragna's orders, a barrage of bullets crashed through the living room window of Virginia's Beverly Hills home. Ben was shot in the head, blowing his eye fifteen feet from his body. Four more bullets crashed into his body, breaking his ribs and tearing up his lungs. Benjamin "Bugsy" Siegel was dead at age 42. Slumping over in a pool of crimson blood drained from his temple and mid section, Ben's one remaining eye was fixated in a blank stare.

One of the shots ripped through the coat sleeve of Al Smiley.

Al yelled to Chick, who was upstairs with his girlfriend Jerri, to douse the lights. Shortly after the gunfire stopped, Chick made his way downstairs to the living room. He slowly turned on the lights. Al was inside the fireplace. Ben was sitting on the floral couch, his head rolled back and his neck resting against the back of the couch, his necktie covered in blood.

Ben's murder was never solved. Many hours were spent by the Beverly Hills police investigating the case. The police were convinced Ben was killed by his own associates who believed Ben or his girlfriend, Virginia Hill, were skimming money from the six million dollar Flamingo Casino Hotel.

Mickey Cohen, Ben's right-hand man in building the Flamingo, reacted violently to Ben's murder. Cohen immediately went to the Hotel Roosevelt, where he believed the killers were staying. Cohen fired rounds from his two .45 caliber semi-automatic handguns into the lobby ceiling and demanded that the assassins meet him outside in ten minutes. No one appeared, and Mickey fled when the police arrived.

* * *

Ben's dream began on a summer day in 1945 while driving his 1942 Super 8 180 Darrin Convertible Victoria, on the way back to Los Angeles from Vegas. Ben always liked riding in style. The 42 Super 8 180 Darrin Convertible Victoria was a fine example of American auto-engineering and design.

Mounted under its bonnet was an L-Head eight cylinder engine that displaced 356 cubic-inches and produced 165 horsepower. It had a three-speed manual transmission and four-wheel hydraulic brakes.

The Packard 180 convertible was the only convertible Victoria to feature a three-position convertible top – meaning the top could be completely closed, completely open or partially open. Only fifteen were assembled in 1942 before WWII put a halt to production. They were owned by the wealthy celebrities of the day, particularly the Hollywood crowd.

Ben argued with Virginia as Mickey sat in the back seat, "Why the hell did we go to that dump," Virginia nagged at Ben. She sat next to him.

Ben yelled back to Mickey, "Mickey, tell her how much fucking money that hellhole brings in." Ben swerved the car to avoid hitting tumbleweed as they passed the Frontier and El Rancho Vegas motels.

"These motels are at the city's edge," Ben said. He continued, "Both motels are wayside inns, unpretentious, built like oversized western ranch houses. They're the best the strip has to offer bored and weary travelers as they voyaged across this god forsaken land back to California!"

At the time, Vegas had a population of 10,000 and new homes were just beginning to be built in the suburb of North Las Vegas. Las Vegas was a cowpoke town where gambling was the Saturday night entertainment for ranchers, prospectors, and workers from nearby Boulder. Prostitution was legal and most of the gambling joints, including the Golden Nugget and Frontier Club, were clustered within the two block radius of Fremont and Second Street.

Reno, on the other hand, was located at the other end of the

State, and attracted the high rollers. Ben knew, given the chance, he could lure those suckers with their deep pockets to Vegas.

Suddenly, about seven miles outside of the city, Virginia screamed out, "Stop the car!" Ben brought the car to an immediate stop, glaring at her. Mickey, having nowhere to go, just kept looking forward trying to ignore the whole situation.

"Now what? We're in the middle of fucking nowhere?" Ben exclaimed. As he got out of the car he started yelling at Virginia. "You fucking bitch. What the hell is your problem? Why did you have me stop in the middle of nowhere? I should make you get out and let you rot in this place."

Virginia was unable to speak. She had a panic attack recalling a flashback of the beating a previous lover had given to her. After a few moments, she regained her composure. She sat in the car and gave it right back to him.

Ben started walking off the hot sweltering road and into the barren desert. There was nothing around but a broken-down motel and sand - lots of sand – not a tree in sight. Mickey got out of the car and started following Ben, "Where you going? There's nowhere here to take a leak."

Ben was staring straight ahead. Slowly, he looked around and smiled. Ben was having an epiphany. The desert heat was making him see illusions of grandeur. He returned to the car, focused on one thing only - building his vision.

"This is the spot," he pronounced. "This is the spot where I am going to build a first class hotel with a big pool and garden. I'm going to call it 'Ben Siegel's Flamingo.' I bet we can get this property for a few nickels and dimes. We're going to make Reno look like a truck stop."

Virginia, now that she had calmed down, said "What the hell are you talking about, Ben?"

"Ben Siegel's Flamingo," was all Ben said. The three of them drove back to Los Angles without much more chatter. Virginia and Mickey knew Ben well enough to leave him alone when he was having one of his "moments."

Upon returning to Los Angeles, Ben's only focus was building his dream, now named "The Flamingo Hotel and Casino." Nothing else mattered to him, not even knowing Virginia was carrying his child.

Moe Sedway, acting as a front for Ben, purchased Margaret Folsom's little motel and the thirty acres of land it was sitting on for "a few nickels and dimes" as Ben predicted. A few months later, Moe quitclaimed that same property to a young Los Angeles attorney named Greg Bautzer, who was drawn into the scheme by Ben. Bautzer in turn, deeded the land to the Nevada Projects Corporation.

Ben and Virginia agreed that she would lay low, remaining out of sight until after the birth of the baby. The press never got wind that the infamous Benjamin Siegel had a child with the Flamingo - - Virginia Hill. No one knew except Chick, Virginia's younger brother. Ben didn't give much thought to the baby or about being a parent again since he already had his "baby" - - the Flamingo.

Two days before he was shot, Ben and Virginia argued about the "other" two million dollars she'd stashed. The money belonged mostly to Meyer Lansky and some of the other crime families from back East. They also fought again about her giving their baby up for adoption. In the end, the baby was given up for adoption to a couple she had just met through her brother, Chick.

Ben, seeing Virginia had her suitcases packed, demanded, "Where the hell are you going?"

"I'm going to Paris. I've never been there and I want to spend summer in Paris!" she exclaimed.

"You're not going," he said.

Virginia stiffened. She looked around the room to where Chick was sitting on a sofa, then to Ben who stood opposite. "Who do you think you are?" she said challenging Ben. "You don't own me, Benjamin Siegel."

Virginia motioned to Chick, "C'mon, to hell with him and this whole goddamn place." She handed her suitcases to Chick as the two left the house. Ben made no attempt to stop her. He just stood by the window looking out at the pool.

*   *   *

Chick met Martha and Stewart Benjamin, the new parents of the baby, at the Brown Derby on Wilshire Boulevard by chance. Chick knew his sister and Ben were not going to be good parents because of their constant fighting and bickering. It was Chick who introduced Virginia to Martha and Stewart Benjamin. Virginia and Ben frequently dined at the Brown Derby bar. There was also the famous incident where Errol Flynn and Virginia got drunk and caused a fight at the Brown Derby.

Despite Virginia and Ben's reputations for being tied to the mob, Chick was very persuasive assuring Martha and Stewart that not only would they be taken care of financially, but no one, absolutely no one, would ever know the truth about the adoption. Chick had not even told his fiancée, Jeri, about the adoption.

After much deliberation and careful thought, Martha, desperate to be a mother, agreed with Stewart to go through with the adoption.

Ben was mad as hell about the money being hidden, especially since he had vehemently defended Virginia when Lansky and Mickey broached the subject of Virginia's Swiss bank account and the missing two million dollars. It didn't seem to bother him that much, though, he'd had a daughter, Valentina. For Ben, Valentina was just an after-thought. Virginia, however, knew it was best for Valentina to be safe. At this time in their lives, neither of them was capable of loving anyone except themselves, not even their own child.

Ben was wrong about many things, but the one thing he got right was the Flamingo and Las Vegas. He called Vegas "Dream Town." One wonders if he knew how close he was to seeing his dream come true. Today, "Las Vegas" means a thousand different things to a thousand different people. For some, Vegas is a dream come true, for others, it's a nightmare.

*　*　*

By the time 1950 rolled around, Ben had been dead for three years. Virginia had a new life, husband, and another child named Peter. Looking back, she wished things had gone differently, but she believed you can't change things that are meant to be. Ben was destined to be his own worst enemy, dying for his dreams. Ben cared more for his casino than money or their child. Reflecting back, Virginia knew Ben was a good parent to his other two daughters, Millicent and Barbara, despite the fact that he rarely saw them. She knew it was Ben's passion for the movies that brought him to Hollywood in the first place. As much a bitch as Virginia could be, she was sad that Ben was shot just before Millicent and Barbara were able to see him. They had planned to spend the summer with Ben.

Virginia died broke in March, 1966 at the tender age of 49. Her body was found near a brook in Koppl, Austria. After several attempts, she finally succeeded in committing suicide. Unlike the other times, on this occasion no one was around to save her. Although her death was ruled as a suicide, it was largely assumed that she was murdered by the crime families.

Chapter 1: April 21, 1968.

Valentina Benjamin, born on February 14, 1947, was a young woman of twenty-one. Val was petite, barely reached 5'4," and weighed less than 115 pounds. She had a slender build with muscular tone. With her light blue eyes, sandy blond hair and ready smile, she was a smart young lady with a quick wit and she knew how to take care of herself. Val was pretty and could easily catch a man's eye. However, she was not as feminine, gorgeous, or glamorous as her biological mother, Virginia Hill. On this day, she rushed around her sparsely furnished apartment, getting ready for work.

Sleeping on the sofa was Val's roommate, Annette Gerrard, who was oblivious to Valentina's racket. Annette was still wearing her tie-dye shirt and red mini-skirt from the night before. Her black go-go boots lay next to the sofa as if she had flung them off without much consideration where they landed.

"Annette, you need to get up. You're going to be late for your audition," Val said to her in a loud authoritative voice.

Groggily, Annette peered through squinting eyes over a pillow held in front of her face and responded, "What?"

Val, still moving about the apartment, said, "I said it's time to rise and shine."

Annette stretched her hands above her head, wiggled her nose and curled her lip. She replied back in a soft, cutesy voice, "Oh my, is it today already?"

"You got in late again, I assume," Val returned.

Although dressing like a teenager, wearing bell bottom jeans and a button down pastel green cotton shirt, Valentina was older and had a job. She worked for MGM Studios in their Special Effects department as an artist. She was highly skilled in both mold making and demolitions. Starting at the age of eight, Valentina's fixation had been blowing things up. Her father, Mr. Stewart Benjamin, was not discouraged by his daughter's interest, and was responsible for guiding her to this productive career – working in special effects.

A studio job in Hollywood was nearly impossible to get without experience. Even people with much more experience did not get the chance to work in one of the studios. To get a job at the MGM Studio, one needed to have "friends" in the industry. Though Val's father worked as an engineer, he had a union friend who worked at the studio - a friend who pulled some strings to get her a job. Proving her skills without having a portfolio did not deter her; she had the demolition skills the studio needed.

Val never had a desire to work in the film industry. It was just a matter of chance that her father connected her with a strong union person. Despite her non-conforming demeanor, she was a responsible young lady, and lived contradictory to the somewhat irrational times surrounding her, relevant especially to sex, drugs and rock-n-roll.

Her roommate, Annette, on the other hand was a lazy party girl who wanted to be an actress but did not want to put the effort into getting parts. Annette would rather "sleep" her way to the top.

Annette had grown up in a small town near Chicago called Munster, Indiana and moved to Hollywood to be an actress nearly three years earlier. Annette was not about to attend college as her parents wished. She was a tall, long-legged, gorgeous woman with deep blue eyes, brunette hair and a smile that could melt any man's heart. Knowing she could get a man to do anything she wanted with the bat of her eyes and the toss of her hair, Annette was successful at getting small roles in B-films.

"Come on Annette, you've got an audition today. I can't keep asking favors for you if you're not going to make an effort to get your ass out of bed."

Putting the final touches of make-up on her perfectly round face, Annette retorted, "Come on Val, you know I'm doing my best. Besides, the producers would rather I get my ass 'in bed.' I'm not as picky as you are."

Val, not in the mood to spar verbal insults with her roommate that morning, ignored the comment.

Five minutes later Annette was dressed. She was looking what she figured was sexy and was ready to go. "Okay Val, I'm ready," she said with a slight smirk on her face.

Annette, having slept with the producer, already knew she would get the role; it was just a matter of formalizing it.

Chapter 2:

Attorney Sam Shaw woke up with a raging headache. He had too many drinks on the red eye from Chicago the previous night. He was on the job, however, and dragged himself out of bed and dressed. Sam was a man in his late forties, and he was fit. This morning he groggily dressed himself in a fashionable black business suit, with a white shirt and colorful blue floral tie.

Employed at the law firm of Thornton, Mender and Bigelow, Sam had been instructed to locate Valentina Benjamin and deliver an envelope that had been in his firm's care for more than 18 years. The envelope had been kept safely tucked away in the firm's safe since 1950. No one, absolutely no one, except for Mr. Nathaniel Thornton, one of the firms's founding partners, and Sam knew about the envelope, and only Thornton knew what was inside. Since 1950 the envelope had only been taken from the safe and replaced a few times by the firm's client.

The envelope had strange markings on the front - a Florentine F with each card suit - a spade, diamond, club, and heart - surrounding the F in a diamond shape. All Sam cared about was that after being told about the envelope and entrusted with its protection more than 18 years ago as a junior attorney, he could finally complete this assignment as requested by Mr. Thornton.

Nothing really seemed to matter to Sam right now, however, except returning home to Chicago to be with his family. Sam had sat on the plane the night before with recurring thoughts of never seeing his family again. No matter how he twisted his mind and thought of different options and possibilities for this trip, the eventuality of what might occur – that he might not return - remained the same. It was an illusion, perhaps, that he could not pin point, but understood well enough.

Sam was going to attempt to deliver the envelope to Valentina that morning at her apartment. Over sleeping because of his late arrival and heavy drinking, he was unable to do so. Sam spotted Val's red 1966 Mustang as she pulled out of her apartment complex driving Annette to the audition. Driving a black Lincoln is hardly inconspicuous in Hollywood traffic, he thought to himself. He tailed her closely, however, waiting for the right opportunity. As Sam followed Val, he had a suspicion that he, too, was being followed. He tried to convince himself it was just his imagination, possibly a result of too much alcohol the night before, but he could not shake the feeling. He reminded himself there was no reason to be paranoid; all he was doing was delivering an envelope. It was a package that had been secret for a long time, and for whatever reason, gave him the willies. Sam watched as Valentina drove into the MGM back lot. He noticed her wave to the security guard as she pulled her convertible through the security gate and disappeared.

The first-generation Ford Mustang was the original pony car manufactured by Ford Motor Company. Val's 66 Mustang debuted with moderate trim changes including a new grille, side ornamentation, wheel covers and gas cap. It had a cherry red exterior, white leather bucket seats, an AM/eight-track sound system, and one of the first AM/FM mono automobile radios. Val was singing along with "I'm a

Believer" by the Monkees. The Mustang convertible was the best-selling car in 1966, with 72,119 sold, beating the number two Impala by almost 2:1.

Meanwhile, a man driving a black Mercedes 280 SL convertible, wearing black pants and black polo shirt, pulled over at a nearby phone booth. Lifting his sunglasses off his nose so he could dial, he glanced around to make certain no one was watching. The man had been tailing Sam since he left his hotel room. Speaking into the phone he inquired of the person at the other end of the line, "Do Flamingos lay eggs?" The voice on the other end replied, "Yeah, why?"

The man in the phone booth said, "Because one just hatched."

"Are you absolutely certain it's her?" the other voice asked.

"No doubt about it. What do you want me to do?"

The deep voice on the telephone grumbled, "Take whatever means necessary to get me what I want. Do I make myself clear?"

"Yes, perfectly," was the response as the phone on the other end hung up.

Chapter 3:

Valentina parked in front of the special effects area. As Val exited her vehicle, she was aware just how beautiful the weather was in Southern California. This was just a typical day. The sky was blue and not a cloud was in sight. The sun was shining and the temperature was a refreshing 78 degrees.

Val was one of only a handful of special effects personnel for MGM who worked on Stanley Kubrick's *2001: A Space Odyssey*. Her new assignment was working on the Star Trek TV series. She was thinking, "Beam me up, Scotty," would make a perfect bumper sticker and started laughing out loud.

Nearly running up a small flight of concrete stairs into the special effects office, Val was unknowingly being watched, not by one person, but by two. Val entered through the office door, almost knocking her boss, Artimis Sylver, on his butt. Artimis, a young man in his late twenties with a lean, muscular physique, was carrying two cups of coffee with a cigarette dangling from his lips.

"Hold on there, Miss B. What's the hurry - you're already late."

Val, not stopping to make idle conversation said, "I know, had to drop Annette off at an audition."

"Another one?" Artimis asked.

Artimis followed Val into the office as Val said, "She'll be fine."

Artimis shot back a quick verbal barb, "Yeah, if she's sober and if she--"

Val was not in the mood for Artimis' feelings toward Annette, "Hey! You're not one to talk mister."

Promptly Artimis changed the direction of the conversation, "I brought you coffee."

Val looked at the two cups of coffee held by Artimis, and replied, "Thanks. Like, that will get you off the hook."

Artimis and Val had gone out on a date the evening before. The date did not go as well for Artimis as he had hoped. "I guess you're still talking to me then," Artimis said.

Val was in a bitch of a mood. This was, as much, from dealing with Annette that morning as last night's tryst with Artimis. She quipped back, "I said, thanks."

Artimis not wanting to let the subject drop said, "After a dinner, a movie and roses, all I get is thanks'?"

Val, being as quick witted as Artimis, countered back, "I barely ate and the movie was boring." After a second but before Artimis could respond, she said, "And I don't like white roses. Who gives a date *white roses* anyway?"

Artimis was Val's supervisor but really wanted to be her "boyfriend," too. Val was not all that interested in Artimis. He was good looking, though not handsome, 6'2", and well toned for a 28-year old. He had sandy brown hair and soft blue eyes that could pierce through most women. Val, however, was of the opinion that she was not like most woman. She was not interested in being with the hip crowd, in particular.

"Well, next time -" Artimis was in mid sentence when Val interrupted, "There won't be a next time."

Artimis moved toward their desks and set the cups of coffee

down. He looked straight at Val with intense eyes and asked, "Why?"

Val picked up one of the cups of coffee from the desk and told Artimis in a firm voice, "Because I don't think it's a good idea for me to be dating my boss."

Artimis reached down to pick up his cup of coffee. He gestured as if making a toast and said, "Teammate. Not boss. Besides, Annette doesn't have a problem dating her bosses if you know what I mean?"

"Whatever," Val replied back.

Artimis sipped his coffee, looked at Val and, in his most sincere voice, he said, "I find you to be one hip, groovy chick and I am smitten with you."

Val did not buy Artimis' line for a second. She chillingly responded, "You just want sex like every other man I've met."

Artimis realized he was losing in this conversation and said without thinking, "No, really, I love you . . ."

Val was too smart and street-wise for her age. She glanced at Artimis and with a devilish grin said, "You love anyone with a vagina."

Artimis lightened up, had a smile from ear to ear and replied, "Hey, I'm a loving kinda guy."

Val sipped from her coffee cup, looked at Artimis and reminded him, "I said one date; you had your date, and now let's just move on." Val set her cup of coffee on the desk and sat down in her black leather office chair to start to work.

Artimis sat at his desk and said, "I can't. This is different."

Val began looking through the script of the movie that they

were preparing the special effects for and said, without looking up, "How so?"

Artimis stared straight at Val and continued the conversation, "Because you're different. I've never known a girl with a tattoo before. Especially one that doesn't drink, refuses to smoke a joint, doesn't smoke cigarettes, and is smart."

At this time, Val was frustrated and tired of the discussion. She only wanted to do her job and get through the day without being harassed by her boss. "It's a birthmark, and flattery won't work. I really might slap your face, but I don't want to give you the satisfaction of my skin touching you."

The conversation was interrupted by a knock at the door. It slowly opened and Sam Shaw entered the room. "I'm looking for a Valentina Benjamin. The security guard told me I could find her here."

Val, with a defiant voice, fired back, "Who wants to know?"

Attorney Shaw showed no intimidation and, with a tongue just as sharp, snarled back, with a tone of indifference, "I do, if you're her." Backing down and softening up, Val acknowledged she was Valentina Benjamin.

"Sam Shaw. I'm with Thornton, Mender and Bigelow, a law firm out of Chicago." Sam stepped to the desk and slowly reached into his pocket. He fidgeted for just a moment before finally pulling out a business card. With a degree of confidence and certainty, he handed it to Val.

She looked at it and asked, "So what do you want with me?"

Unlocking and slowly opening his leather attaché case, Sam

removed the large manila envelope. "I have something for you."

Artimis, under his breath, murmured, "So do I."

Before Sam removed the envelope from the brief case, he instructed Val to show him the back of her left shoulder.

"What the hell for?" she demanded.

"I need to make certain that you are the person for whom this is intended." Sam, pointing to the open brief case stated, "That envelope has been in our office for quite some time. I'm instructed to make certain that the marking on the front of this envelope matches the person's birthmark. Now let's have a look -see."

For some inexplicable reason, Artimis blurted out, "Why do you want to see her tattoo?"

Without turning to acknowledge Artimis's question, Sam reached suddenly across the desk and pulled down Val's tie-dye T-shirt just enough to look at her left shoulder. With a smirk he muttered and said, "My, my, oh my," when he saw the birthmark was the same as the markings on the envelope. Handing Val the envelope, he moved towards the door quietly telling Val, "Have a nice life." Sam turned abruptly to leave.

As he was leaving, Val yelled out, "Thanks, I think?"

Sam exited through the door, satisfied that he had accomplished his mission.

Sam walked towards the black Lincoln, smiling to himself. Finally, after all these years the firm was free of the envelope that for some inexplicable reason had tormented him all these years. Sam did not know why that envelope bothered him so much. All he knew was that for whatever reason it gave him a weird sensation of gloom and doom - - almost like it was cursed. The only thing Sam cared about now was that after all these years he was finally able to complete the assignment requested by Mr. Thornton. Thornton told Sam he was the only person in the firm he could trust with the knowledge of the envelope at the time Thornton hired him.

Thornton's client had ties with Chicago. Thornton knew he could not trust the other attorneys in the firm because he never knew for certain where their loyalties laid. Especially since Thornton's client was connected with the Chicago families.

Sam never asked about the contents of the envelope. But whatever it was, Thornton was the only person who knew the client and the contents of the damn thing. It was his sixth sense that gave him an eerie feeling about it, and he wanted no part of it or even knowing its contents.

Now, it was delivered and nothing else mattered except returning to Chicago to be with his family.

Sam, for some inexplicable reason, was sweating profusely, wiping his brow with a silk handkerchief. Sam's sixth sense gave him a sickening feeling in the pit of his stomach that all was not what it should be. A mindless fear gripped Sam as he began to open his car door. A bald man dressed in mechanic's garb walked by, with an air of foreboding and strangeness about him. The mechanic flashed a gruesome smile showing perfectly white teeth with large spaces between them as he passed. As he moved on away he said with a strong, yet gentle voice, "Have a nice day, Mr. Shaw."

Sam muttered back, "You, too."

Sam slid into the driver's seat of the black Lincoln Town car. Sam turned on the radio, put the car into drive and pulled out of the back lot. Passing through the security gate, Sam waved to the guard. The guard nodded and waved back. From the passenger seat, Sam picked up a pack of Lucky Strike cigarettes, tapped the pack against his hand, took out a cigarette and put it in his mouth. He pushed the cigarette lighter into the walnut finished dash and looked back through the rear view mirror. As he did so, he thought to himself, "How the hell did that mechanic, a complete stranger, know my name?" As the coil of the cigarette lighter began to turn red hot, a slightly noticeable fermented odor of noxious fumes wafted throughout the Town car.

Before he could give it a thought, the car exploded in a fireball, sending metal and pieces of Sam into the clear blue sky.

As the metal fragments came crashing down, Artimis and Val, along with several other studio employees, rushed outside to see what had caused such a thunderous explosion. They opened the door, and no sooner did they emerge to sunlight when gunshots crackled through the air. Val was directly behind Artimis, clutching his belt loop. Her normally calm complexion was flushed red with a mixture of excitement and surprise as the concrete walls around them were peppered with bullets, and windows began breaking. Then she realized they were the ones being shot at.

Artimis, without hesitation, covered Val with his body to shield her, simultaneously throwing her and himself back inside the doorway and slamming it behind them. For a moment, the shooting stopped.

Artimis peeked out the window to try and see what was happening. When the shooting stopped, more people began to come out of nearby offices into the back lot.

Breathing heavily, Artimis made sure Val was unhurt and said in a half comical voice, "Now that's what I call a special delivery."

Val unfazed by the situation looked at Artimis and said, "Don't you ever throw me around like that again."

Artimis, who was still breathing heavily, looked at her in disbelief and said, "As opposed to getting shot!" Artimis suspected Val was one tough cookie, but even he was surprised that Val was not rattled by the shooting.

"How do you know they were shooting at me? Maybe it's one of your jilted lovers," said Val.

"Because it's that stupid envelope and I don't have any jilted lovers." Artimis grabbed the envelope from Val's hand. Val did not have time to even look at the damn thing before the explosion. Looking at the envelope, Artimis realized that the markings on the envelope were the exact same as Val's tattoo.

Shoving the front of the envelope in her face he said, "Do you think this is a coincidence? Look, this design is the same as your tattoo or birthmark, whatever you want to call it."

"Give me that!" Val shouted as she grabbed the envelope from Artimis' hand.

Artimis did not resist when Val took the envelope from him. "If I didn't know better, I'd say that envelope is bad for your health," he said.

Val looked at Artimis straight in his face almost nose to nose, "Ya think?"

Artimis stared back at Val and said, "Why are you being such a bitch?"

"I don't know. I'm sorry. You just have a knack of rubbing me the wrong way. You're right. I should be thankful to you for pulling me out of the line of fire."

Artimis replied, "Apology accepted."

In time, several black and white patrol cars and red ambulances with lights blinking and sirens blaring pulled into the back lot. They tried to contain the area while keeping the growing crowd at bay.

The bald mechanic, meanwhile, was at a telephone booth five blocks away and two blocks over, making a call. "Hey, it's me. I got Shaw but missed the girl . . . I know, I understand . . . No. I'm sure I can handle it . . . consider it done."

Not wanting to be questioned by the cops, Artimis and Val snuck out of the office and made their way off the back lot in Artimis' car, a cobalt blue '65 Corvette Stingray Coupe. Artimis suggested the two of them stay at his place until things settled down. Val didn't put up much of an argument but insisted they stop by her apartment, prior to going to his place. Artimis, delighted at the prospect of Val being his house guest, was ecstatic, and agreed with her request. There was a commotion of squad cars and emergency personnel flocking through the front security gate, but the guard at the back exit, paid little attention to Artimis driving off the premises. He and Val did so a midst a line of studio escapees.

Val and Artimis walked quickly through the courtyard of Val's apartment complex. The complex, lined with mature palm trees, was located on the corner of North Serrano and Fernwood. As Val fumbled for her keys, her landlady, Mona Johnson, an older woman with a rat's nest of red hair piled up on her head, wearing fly-eye glasses, holding her tiny, nervous toy poodle under one arm and her ever present cigarette in her free hand, shouted out in an irritated voice, "Miss Benjamin?"

Annoyed, Val called back, "Yes, Miss Johnson."

Moving quickly toward Val and Artimis, Ms. Johnson said, "I wanna talk to you."

Val finally found her keys and put the key into the door lock, replied; "Not now Miss Johnson, I'm in a bit of a hurry."

Ms. Johnson had caught up with Val and was now standing directly behind her. "Not so fast, you're always in a hurry. What kinda business are you in anyway? Are you turning tricks in there? Damned movie people . . ."

Val stood half way inside her apartment and replied, "Don't be ridiculous."

Miss Johnson pointed her bony finger at Val's face, "Men comin' and goin' . . ."

Artimis hearing this tidbit of information snickered out loud and said "Do tell."

"Shut up," Val snapped. She flashed an angry defiant look towards Artimis.

Miss Johnson, whose cigarette was now in complete ashes,

continued her interrogation of Val and said, "I run a respectable place here missy. So who were those men that were here earlier? . . . 'bout scared me to death. I threatened to call the police on them if they wouldn't leave."

Val tried to close the front door of her apartment in Miss Johnson's face and replied, "I don't know . . . can we talk about this later?"

Miss Johnson stuck her left foot out to keep the front door from closing and said, "Sure we can . . . we can also discuss your rent - - you're late!"

Val opened the door as wide as it would go, and said loudly, "I am not! Check your fuckin' mail box."

Mona flicked the cigarette from her hand onto the sidewalk in front of Val's door, turned and walked off murmuring to herself. Then she pulled a joint from her pocket, and lighting it, she turned to face Val, took a hit and said, "Want a toke?"

Val said, "No thanks," and closed the door.

She and Artimis were shocked as they looked at her apartment. The sparsely furnished apartment was ransacked with everything thrown about. What little pieces of furniture Val and Annette had were tipped over, and papers littered the place everywhere.

Artimis realizing the gravity of the situation asked dryly, "Annette entertaining again last night?"

"No that was me letting out my frustration after our date."

Val quickly gathered a few items of clothing, her tooth brush, and other personal items, and tossed them in a suitcase. She jotted a note to Annette telling her that she would be out of town for a few weeks on a shoot. Val and Artimis took the time to tidy up and then they were out the door and on their way to his place.

As they entered Artimis' apartment, Val noticed it was a typical bachelor pad with red and chocolate brown bean bag chairs, a small kitchen table with four chairs, a sofa, a waterbed, and a color Zenith television. Val tossed her suitcase on the sofa and flopped down on a red bean bag chair.

Val stared at the envelope, not quite sure what to make of the markings that were exactly the same as her birthmark. She cautiously opened the envelope and took out an aging letter, three bundles of cash, some photos and four playing cards - all queens. Each queen was a different suit and each was from a different casino. The Queen of Hearts was from the Flamingo, the Queen of Spades was from the Sands, the Queen of Clubs was from the Dunes, and the Queen of Diamonds was from the Sahara.

"Let's see, a bundle of cash – all 100 dollar bills," Val murmured as she skimmed through the money. Her eyes widened with the flip of each bill and she estimated there was about $30,000. "Four Queens, a few black and white photos of people she did not know, and a letter to get me almost dead. Nice."

Val did not pay attention to the distinctions of each of the cards nor did she realize at first that they were from different casinos.

Bee playing cards were the brand most often used by a casino followed by Bicycle. First manufactured by Consolidated-Dougherty in 1892, they bore the number "92" on the Ace of Spades.

Bee playing cards had a diamond back, typically blue or red, though casinos frequently used customized Bee cards featuring their particular logo on the back. Unlike Bicycle cards, Bee had borderless backs, making the facing of any card that was even partially revealed clearly visible. The diamond back of the card was also very regular and low-profile compared to other back designs, which simplified "bottom-dealing" and other forms of cheating.

The Queen of Hearts from the Flamingo had a red diamond back with a small flamingo logo added. The Queen of Spades from the Sands was a blue diamond back design with Sands written across the back in script. The Queen of Clubs from the Dunes was also a blue diamond back design with Dunes written in an octagon shaped box on the back. The Queen of Diamonds was a red diamond back design Bicycle playing card with Sahara written across in script.

Val began to read the letter out loud. "My darling daughter, by the time you get this letter, if you ever do, I'll probably be long gone." "What the hell?" exclaimed Valentina clearly becoming distraught. Continuing she read, "Please read this letter carefully and most importantly don't let anyone know you have the cards. Things are not always what they seem. Such is your legacy. The Four Queens are four ladies that will lead you to a fortune, and your true identity."

Artimis interrupted, "So, you're not who you think you are?"

"This is serious," Val said without taking offense.

Artimis looked sternly at Val as she sat and said, "Yeah, I don't see the humor in exploding cars and bullets flying at me. Movies yes, especially when *we* set the explosions. Everyday life, " he let it trail off.

* * *

Finishing the letter, Val read:

*My dear darling daughter by the time you get this
letter, if you ever do, I will probably be long gone. Please read
this letter carefully and most importantly, don't let anyone know
you have the cards. Things are not always what they seem to
be. Such is your legacy. The four queens are four ladies that
will lead you to a fortune, and your true identity.*

*Your journey begins with the Queen of Hearts
followed by the Queen of Clubs, Spades and finally the Queen
of Diamonds. The photos with this letter are mementos I
wanted you to have to remember your father and I. Some may
or may not be of importance to your journey - - only you will be
able to decide.*

Love Mom

Artimis looked at the queens Val was holding in her lap as she
finished reading the letter. "What does the writing on the cards say?"
he asked.

Val looked at the writing on the cards and said, "I'm not sure, it
looks like some riddles. I don't know what the hell is going on. I
spoke to my mom yesterday." Val did not bother to look any closer at
the photos or the cards.

As she carefully folded the letter and placed it back in the
envelope with the cards and photos, she put the cash in her purse and
said with a defiant voice, "I gotta go see my mom, now!" Val rose up
from the chair, her face pale, as if - - as if, she had just seen a ghost.

Artimis noticed the look on Val's face and became concerned. He had never seen her act this way before. "Val, what else did the letter say?"

Val moved toward the door in a hyper and anxious manner and said, "It says something about my 'journey begins with the Queen of Hearts." Recovering from her shock and disbelief, Val motioned to Artimis and curtly said, "Let's go!"

Little did she know that she had just entered into a long awaiting nightmare.

Chapter 4:

Jordan Hamilton was puffing on his Por Laranga cigar as he pored over the newspaper that he was reading at his office desk. His office was located on the penthouse floor of Lake Point Tower, a prominent property completed in that year and situated at Lake Shore Drive in Chicago. The best real estate with a view of Chicago's skyline was along the Chicago River, which ran through the city.

As Tony Iannotti entered Jordan's office, he managed a smile despite the sickly sweet tobacco fumes that hung in the air like a thick blanket. The art treasures hanging on the walls were nothing short of magnificent. The bronze statues and elegantly appointed furniture defined the room with a grace fit for royalty.

"Still raining?" asked Jordan.

Iannotti took off his raincoat and hung it on a coat rack by the door. He removed his hat, wiping the raindrops from his face, and replied, "Yea, it's pouring outside."

Jordan noted that Tony was under pressure. Tony, the "protector of Jordan's realm," was an unemotional operator who took care of Jordan's nasty side of business with an undaunted tenacity and a demand for perfection in everyone else but himself. Today his thicket of dark brown hair looked like straw in a crosswind, his eyes moved more than usual, and there were tension lines on his forehead that Jordan had never seen before. Iannotti was in his mid-thirties, tall, and arrogant with something about him menacing. He had a quality of self-control that seemed almost egotistical. His dark eyes and expensive clothing offset by his wildly disheveled hair gave him the appearance of someone that didn't care how he looked.

"I have the latest report," Tony said uneasily. He walked over to Jordan's desk and handed it to him.

Though he was one of the most powerful men in the hierarchy, he still feared the wrath of Jordan. To those on the outside, Jordan had the reputation of being a cold, callous man who had built an empire on being calm, relaxed and in total control. Those on the inside knew a very different person; one who was explosive and irrational. His mood was likely to change as quickly as the Chicago weather. As head of one of the largest Chicago crime syndicates, Jordan lived in a world of delusion and paranoia.

Jordan continued puffing on his cigar. Sitting behind his large Mahogany desk, Jordan pushed the newspaper aside. Jordan's desk was spotless. Other than the newspaper, nothing was on the desk top.

Jordan did not strike you as a man with brilliant intelligence, photographic memory or fluency in five languages. He was 6'0," had an athletic build, and was in his late fifties. He had a healthy head of silvery-gray hair and mesmerizing light brown eyes; he appeared more flamboyant.

Jordan usually found himself amused by the uneasiness that gripped his associates after a failed mission.

"Our man in Los Angeles eliminated attorney Shaw," reported Tony.

Jordan asked, "What about the envelope?" The envelope was the thing Jordan was concerned about. He didn't care much about Shaw or anyone else that might know the contents of it.

Tony's face tightened slightly as he delivered the news of the botched mission: "Shaw delivered it to the girl, but our man blew his assignment. He got carried away and started shooting at her instead of getting the envelope."

The Mechanic, as he was known to those on the inside, had a propensity for killing rather than simply completing what he was told to do. He had a reputation for ensuring there were no loose ends or witnesses. This time was different. He got sloppy, or so Iannotti thought. Jordan, on the other hand, was more suspicious of why the Mechanic did not succeed.

Jordan folded his hands in front of him as Iannotti sat down in the burgundy, leather chair directly across from him.

"Where is she now?" he asked.

Tony was apprehensive as he told Jordan, "We don't know."

Jordan surveyed the room and studied Iannotti's facial expressions. He could see that Tony was nervous for failing to obtain the envelope.

Jordan's voice was unsympathetic as he asked, "What? How can you guys screw up a simple assignment? I don't care what needs to be done, get me that envelope and eliminate anyone you suspect has seen it. If Joe finds out it's still out there, we're all in trouble." Amidst a circle of smoke hanging around his desk, Jordan continued, "Damn Irish Catholics, uglier than the Italians." Iannotti smiled, hiseyes brightened, and he laughed at Jordan's comments.

Joe, a prominent American businessman and political figure was closely tied to the Democratic Party. He was not a person one wanted to be with on the wrong side. During World War I, he was an assistant manager to a major steel producer. Joe became friends with FDR in the 30's. A visionary, he always looked at the forefront of new technology. He made huge profits from reorganizing and refinancing several Hollywood studios. After prohibition ended in 1933, Joe accumulated an even larger fortune when his company became the exclusive import agent for Gordon's Gin and Dewar's Scotch.

Joe, unknown to the public, was also involved with the El Rancho Vegas Casino. It was the first casino on what was currently the Las Vegas, Strip opening on April 3, 1941. El Rancho stood for almost 20 years before mysteriously being destroyed by a fire in 1960. During that time, Joe made a fortune from the casino. Regarding the El Rancho, Bugsy Siegel once said, "Do you know how much fucking money is made from that dump?"

Its success spawned a second hotel, the Hotel Last Frontier, in 1942. Mr. Siegel, realizing how much money was being made under the table at his El Cortez Casino, took interest in the growing gaming center and this led to other casino resorts such as the Flamingo, which opened on December 26, 1946, and the Desert Inn, which opened in 1950. The funding for many of these projects was provided by the American National Insurance Company, which was based in the then notorious gambling empire of Galveston, Texas. Joe used his influence with the Teamsters to fund other "projects" along the Strip.

Jordan knew that Joe would go to great extremes to protect his and his families' reputation from being associated with the mafia. Too much was at stake right now, especially as his son was running in the upcoming elections. This was one assignment that had to be handled correctly and without any further complications.

Jordan stared out of the window at the Chicago skyline. The rain had subsided, but it was still overcast.

"What's our next move?" Jordan asked Tony.

Tony remained seated in his chair. Leaning toward Jordan, Tony rubbed his chin and said, "I have men staking out the girl's parents' home and also men in Vegas in case she surfaces."

Turning away from the window, Jordan moved to the private bar in his office. He picked up a decanter of whiskey. Extending his arm towards Tony, he gestured to him that he was offering him a drink. Tony shook his head, declining the offer. Jordan placed a Baccarat high ball glass on the bar, poured himself a drink and asked, "Do you anticipate any other problems?"

Tony got up from the chair and grabbed his hat and coat. As he was putting on his coat, he quietly responded, "Just one - Mickey is in Vegas."

Jordan sipped the whiskey in his glass, rolled the slightly brownish golden liquid around in the glass, and looked in Tony's direction. Tony was already heading towards the door.

"I see," said Jordan. "We'll handle him if he gets involved."

As Tony left Jordan Hamilton's office, he could tell his boss was worried.

Chapter 5:

Martha, a typical suburban housewife and stay-at-home mom, was comfortable entertaining guests in her home. She usually had a glass of wine in her hand and was somewhat oblivious to reality. Always seeming to be in a cheerful mood, her acting could win her an Oscar with the way she hid her true feelings of despair and frustration.

Her husband, Stewart, an aeronautical engineer, worked for Fairchild and earned $50,000 a year. He worked on special projects in the aerospace division of NASA. Stewart was a middle-aged man with a lot of mileage on his face. Unlike Martha, who still looked youthful despite being in her early fifties, Stewart looked much older than his age. Although his eyes always lit up when he saw Val, he could never truly hide his feeling of remorse knowing Val's biological parents were cold-hearted mobsters. Every now and then he would see a dark side of Val that frightened him.

The Benjamins still resided in the same house that Valentina grew up in as a child. The home was in a nice suburb of Los Angeles; middle class, affluent, but not wealthy. The home was ranch style, approximately 2,500 square feet with an off-white stucco exterior and a faded red Spanish tile roof.

Val and Artimis arrived there in his '65 Corvette Stingray at approximately 6 p.m. Artimis parked his car in the driveway and the two exited with Artimis slightly behind Val. They entered the house through the back door, and Val called out, "Mom, dad, I'm home."

She entered through the kitchen where she saw her mom preparing the evening meal. The always-present glass of wine was on the kitchen island.

"Mom, an attorney delivered this envelope to me at work today. Val's mother did not respond immediately, so Val continued, "After he left there was an explosion and people starting shooting at me."

Without looking at Val or stopping the preparation of her mashed potatoes, Martha replied in a nonchalant, almost clueless manner, "More Vietnam war protesters, dear?"

Val rolled her eyes at her mother's comment. "No, mom, and they weren't rioters over King's death either. Didn't you hear what I said? People were shooting at me."

Martha, in somewhat of a stupor, stopped mashing the potatoes, turned, and looked at Val.

"Well, you look fine to me, dear. Who's your friend?" she Asked, gawking at Artimis.

"He's my boss, mom. Mom this is Artimis, Artimis this is my mother," Val said as she introduced the two to each other.

Standing in the kitchen near the center, granite counter top island, Val pulled out the envelope from under her sweater showing it to Martha. "This envelope contained a letter from my 'mother' saying, "My dear darling daughter, by the time you receive this I will be long gone. It also had about thirty thousand dollars in cash, some photos, and four cards, all queens from different casinos."

The envelope also had a photo of the El Rancho Mirage Casino. Several other photos were of Virginia Hill and Bugsy Siegel, though Val didn't recognize them or know who the other people were in the photos.

"What the hell is going on?" Val said confrontationally.

Martha looked at Stewart, who had just entered the room. "Well," she said in a nervous, shaky voice. "I was praying this day would never come. Stewart cleared his throat, and said, "Val let's sit in the living room." By way of introduction, he nodded to Artimis and then motioned them into the living room.

The room was quaint with classic décor and stylish furniture. Martha sat first on the white cloth sofa and patted it indicating to Val to sit next to her. Artimis and Stewart each sat in the black leather reclining chairs near the sofa. A glass coffee table with a candy dish full of mints and art deco pieces was in front of the sofa. Martha, looking Val straight in the eye said, "You're adopted."

Val, with a stunned expression blurted out, "What?"

Martha began, "When you were an infant, your biological mother asked your father and I to take care of you. It was shortly after your biological father died, that we formally adopted you."

Val, already with tears welling up in her eyes asked, "Mom, who were my parents?"

Martha, with a quiver in her voice, her hands folded neatly in her lap replied, "Have you heard of Bugsy Siegel and Virginia Hill?"

Val looked her mother in the eye and asked, "Who?"

Martha regained her composure and with unequivocal confidence stated, "Your parents were Bugsy Siegel and Virginia Hill, the photos of the people in that envelope." She pointed at the photos in Val's hand.

Almost involuntarily, Artimis uttered, "Whoa." There was a brief silence in the room, and he continued, "Didn't see that one coming."

Val gave him a quick glare that said, "Shut up!" Artimis sat back in his seat as he realized this was not the time or place for jokes or wise cracks.

Val stood up, clutching the envelope. The photos were still on the table. She showed her left shoulder to her mother and asked, "So does this envelope have something to do with my birthmark?" Martha gave a quick glance at the birthmark and then at the envelope. "Yes, I guess it does. Virginia said she hid millions for you. Nobody actually believed her though."

Val put her shirt back over her shoulder and was still standing with the envelope in her left hand as she asked, "Why not?"

Martha looked at Val and said, "Please sit down. You're making me nervous." Val sat back down next to Martha with her head hung low. Martha continued, her eyes stone cold, her voice shallow and iced "Because anyone who knew Virginia knew she was rather selfish and self-centered. She seemed only to be interested in what she could take - never give. I read Virginia ended up broke living in Colorado. I heard she became a recluse after testifying about your father's death before Congress in 1951."

"Why didn't you tell me I was adopted? Val asked. Tears fully formed, now, in the corner of her eyes and began to trickle down her face.

"We were afraid you would search for your biological mother."

Martha trembled as she spoke. "No one knew you were adopted and no one knew two infamous people were your biological parents. I certainly didn't want you to find that out."

Val was still in shock learning she was adopted. Not knowing what to say and still bewildered from the events of the day, she wiped the tears from her face, turned toward her mother, changed the subject and asked, "So these cards are sort of like a treasure map?"

Artimis, seeing an opportunity, joined in the conversation again, "Val, didn't that letter say your journey began with the Queen of Hearts?"

This time Val was not upset with Artimis' interruption and replied in a civil tone, "Yeah, it did."

Val put her hand inside the envelope and removed the letter from the envelope with the four cards, saying, "The Queen of Hearts is from the Flamingo Hotel. The Queen of Clubs is from the Sands, the Queen of Spades is from the El Rancho Casino and the Queen of Diamonds is from the Sahara. She reread the letter.

Val put the letter down and quickly picked up the Queen of Hearts, and read the clue:

> *"Your journey begins at the Heart of Vegas. Help will be waiting in a mysterious way."*

Val hurriedly placed the contents from the envelope back inside and abruptly stood up. Val glanced over at her dad, who had remained silent during Martha's revelation about Val being adopted, and said, "Well, mom, dad, this has been an interesting and enlightening day. I have lots of questions about my being adopted, but for now I'm going to Vegas to find out what's hidden for me."

As Val began to get up from the sofa, Stewart finally spoke, "Martha, you'd better tell her the rest."

Martha glared at Stewart and then grabbed both of Val's hands, looked at her directly and said, "Val, there is one more thing you need to know." Val, staring straight into her mother's eyes, asked, "What's that, mom?"

Without hesitation Martha said, "You have a guardian."

Val pulled her hands away from Martha, backed off, and in a stunned voice said, "I have a what?" Stewart, seeing the look of despair on Martha's face, interjected, "You have a guardian - a person who we have never met who is watching out for you. All we know is that when you wanted something, and we couldn't afford it, money showed up. When there were any problems, whatever it was, it was always taken care of. We didn't ask any questions because of who your biological parents were."

Val looked directly at her father and asked, "You're kidding right, dad?"

Stewart with a serious look said, "I wish I was. When you were an infant, and we took you to the doctor, we never got a bill. When I called to ask how much we owed, the receptionist said that our account had been settled. She said a man came in with cash and paid in full. He said he wished to remain anonymous. This happened with the dentist too. Each time you had an appointment, your bill was always paid by someone with cash."

Joining the conversation, Martha, in an authoritative voice, said,

"Do you remember shopping for your car with your father?" Val nodded yes. Martha continued, "When you got home from the dealership, the sales person called and said that your car was paid for in full and said for your father to pick it up the next day. You asked why we didn't tell you that you were adopted until now. It was terrifying knowing someone was watching you all of the time. "

Artimis interrupted the moment, "I'm going with you to Vegas."

Val, turning her attention to Artimis retorted, "Like hell you are. I don't need your help, and I don't want to put you in harm's way."

Artimis, not wanting to take "no" for an answer responded, "Someone's trying to kill you, so I'm most certainly going with you. Besides, you're going to need my special talents."

"Yeah, what's that?" Val queried.

Artimis boasted, "I have some props I've borrowed from the studio in a storage unit near my apartment that we can use in case your trigger happy friend decides to show up again."

"What kinda 'props'?" Val asked puzzled by his comment.

"I borrowed some props they didn't use in the James Bond movie, thinking I would add them to my 'Vette. I wasn't sure if I would ever outfit my 'Vette with some of the gadgets, but it would be a blast to have my buddy put them on your Mustang."

Val shook her head in amazement, thinking Artimis was out of his mind. She thought arguing with him would be futile, and reluctantly agreed, "Yeah, right. Okay. But no funny business and we get separate rooms."

Artimis, raised his hand in acceptance and said, "Whatever."

Val turned to Martha and Stewart and said in a forceful, yet gentle voice, "Mom, dad, we will finish this conversation later. I want to know more, but for now I want to find answers in Vegas."

Artimis, preparing to leave with Val, said to Martha and Stewart, "Pleasure to meet both of you." As he shook Stewart's hand to say goodbye, he looked at Val and said, "I'll call the office and tell them we will be out of town for a few weeks. Half the studio's probably on vacation anyway. I'll have Ernie outfit your Mustang with the stuff I got in storage while we're gone.

Chapter 6

The harsh sun had set and was replaced by a silver moon. The night air was clear and crisp. From his vantage point high above the city, Mickey Cohen could see the neon lights ebb and flow like theatre marquees when seen from forty stories. It was a picturesque art form from what was only a mound of sand less than 22, years ago, Mickey thought. He wondered if this was what Ben envisioned the day he had his epiphany during their drive back to Los Angeles in 1946.

The sound of a knock at his door intruded on his tranquility. Mickey was the executive vice president and director of archives for the Flamingo Hotel and Casino. He had been employed at the Flamingo since before its rainy opening night in December, 1946.

While in Vegas, his routine never varied. Each evening, he would stand in front of the picture window staring around at what was now an entertainment destination for the Hollywood crowd. He helped build Vegas from the ground up. Following Ben's death he stayed on at the Flamingo as its manager. Mickey was better at handling Meyer Lansky's money than Ben had ever been. For his efforts, he was rewarded handsomely. Mickey shrewdly invested in other local real estate along the strip with Joe, and with the development of other casinos and entertainers such as Frank Sinatra, Dean Martin, Wayne Newton, and Liberace, his profits soared daily.

With an obsession for stylistic and fashionable clothes, Mickey could afford any wardrobe he desired. His closet was the size of a large bedroom with rows of tailored suits hanging on rods. Next to each suit was a monogrammed shirt and tie. Beneath each suit was a pair of shoes, making each ensemble complete. The closet had special lighting to "display" his outfits.

Again, there was a knock at the door to his suite. Without turning, Mickey called out, "Enter." The door slowly opened into the lavish suite which also served as Mickey's office. The mahogany desk was clear except for a solid gold pen set and a framed photo of Ben and Virginia. No expense had been spared in decorating the space. The furnishings had cost upwards of five million dollars. The walls and ceiling were intricately carved and paneled in mahogany, as was most of the furniture. Elegant Persian rugs covered the hardwood floors. The upholstered chairs and couch were accented by original oil paintings and sculptures that looked like they belonged in a museum. Even by Vegas standards, the office was luxurious and opulent.

Michael J. Caldwell, a young attorney personally employed by Mickey, opened the door and made his way inside. The view from the picture windows was nothing short of spectacular. Caesar's Palace was lit up with blue lights. The marble monuments in front of Caesars' appeared life-like, as if from a ghostly past to haunt those who dared to enter its realm. Caldwell, a mid-west transplant with dark intense eyes magnified by his horn rimmed glasses and slender build, stood 5'8". He was professionally dressed in a dark blue suit with a white shirt and red tie. Caldwell looked more like a GQ magazine executive than a Vegas lawyer. Quietly, respectfully, and with great deference he addressed Mickey, "News from LA, sir."

Mickey, still gazing out the window asked, "Any word why Sam would be a target?"

Caldwell was standing next to Mickey. Mickey remained at the window surveying the night sky. "Possibly," said Caldwell.

Mickey slowly turned his undivided attention toward Michael and said, "Okay, what do you know so far?"

Michael faced Mickey, "You're not going to like this, sir."

Mickey smiled, turned, and began to walk away. He looked back at Michael, as he did so and said, "That bad, huh?"

Michael joined Mickey in moving about the room. The room was large enough for the two men to walk as if strolling in a park. As they walked, Michael said, "I got word from Chicago that Joe has been ruffling a few feathers. Jordan Hamilton sent Tony Ianotti to L.A. the same time Sam was hit. According to our sources, Ianotti was nowhere near the scene of the explosion. Our people think the Mechanic was involved, but they're not certain because of how sloppy the hit was handled."

Muttering out loud, Mickey said to himself, "So it begins."

Michael, always paying attention to details, with an inquisitive look on his face asked, "What begins sir?"

Mickey stopped walking and was standing next to his desk. Michael was in front of the desk waiting for Mickey's response. Mickey frowned, rubbed his chin with his index finger and thumb, and said, "Nothing, nothing at all. Just thinking out loud to myself. What else you got?"

Michael continued his report, "According to Sam's legal secretary, Sheila, Thornton met with Sam in private before he left the office. When she asked Sam about the envelope he was carrying, Sam got real quiet and appeared agitated. According to Sheila, Sam hastily opened his brief case and put the envelope inside it. He told her to book the next flight to LA for him and then he left for the airport."

Mickey placed his hand on the desk and glanced at the photo of Ben and Virginia. "Someone else knows about that envelope and its contents. Thornton is the only person who knows exactly what's inside. I only have a suspicion, damn her."

Michael, confused by Mickey's comments about the envelope, asked, "What envelope and who is the *she* you're talking about sir?"

Mickey slowly turned toward Michael and with a brooding look, grimly said, "The less you know right now, the better it will be for your safety. I need you to do a title search on the El Rancho Mirage. When you're finished with the title search, get me as much information on the fire that destroyed it, the insurance pay out, and whatever else you can dig up." Mickey now spoke as a drill sergeant barking out orders, "Oh, and make certain no one and I mean absolutely no one knows what you're doing. If anybody starts asking questions, call me. You got it?"

"Yes," said Michael. "Anything else?"

Mickey, still in deep thought just said, "Yea, see if you can get yourself hired at Thornton's firm in Chicago. It might help if you were inside that firm for now." Caldwell fiendishly smiled at Mickey's suggestion because he'd already been approached by Thornton to join the firm.

Chapter 7

As the sun was fading, the sky's pale shades of orange and pink with grey puffy clouds was a sight to behold. No photo or painting could capture the true essence of the magnificent vista. Val and Artimis were not paying attention to Nature's beautiful fading light surrounding them. Instead, they were in a taxi, arguing about the meaning of what was the Heart of Vegas.

Robert Wentworth, the driver of the Yellow Checker taxi, had been listening to Val and Artimis argue from the time he picked them up at McCarran Airport throughout the drive from one casino to another. He was always asked to "wait" while the two went inside, only to come back out within a few minutes.

Val, frustrated with their lack of progress, harshly said, "Okay smart ass, we're in downtown Vegas and nobody seems to know anything about this damn Queen of Hearts card."

Artimis poignantly said, "We need to keep asking around. The letter said, 'Your journey begins at the Heart of Vegas. Help will be waiting in a mysterious way.' Somebody has to know something about this card."

"So what makes you think the Heart of Vegas is in downtown Vegas?" asked Val.

Artimis, in a smug voice declared, "Because it makes sense. The Four Queens refers to the four cards. There are four hotels, one on each of the corners at the same intersection as the Four Queens on Fremont Street."

The cab driver looked over his shoulder and told Val and

Artimis, "You two are both frickin' idiots. Anyone who knows anything about Vegas knows that the Heart of Vegas is the Flamingo Hotel."

Val glanced at the driver and said, "What? What do you mean the Heart of Vegas is the Flamingo?"

The cabbie began by saying, "Bugsy Siegel built the place in 46. He came over to Vegas from L.A. one day and took a look around. He had an idea to build a luxury hotel and casino and got a lot of *other* people's money to invest. Vegas was wide open with legalized gambling and cat houses. Bugsy saw the possibilities and moved right in. He stayed with it until June, 1947 when *they* filled his head with so many bullets that the cops never found all the pieces."

Val's stomach churned and she was suddenly squeamish. Knowing her biological father was the infamous Bugsy Siegel, she was becoming ill at hearing the details of his death. Not wanting to hear any more, Val cut-off the cabbie and said, "Take us to the Flamingo."

As the cabbie drove to the Flamingo, he continued his story saying, "And here's the Sahara, built on the strip in '52. It was the sixth resort to open here on the Strip. Did you know that in 1964 The Beatles stayed at the Sahara and played two shows at the Convention Center?"

"Over here is the Sands, also built in 52. The Sands was the seventh resort to open on the Strip. Howard Hughes purchased the joint just a few years ago. He had that architect - what's his name, oh yeah, Martin Stern, Jr., and the five hundred room circular tower last year. Let me tell you, plenty of coin behind that one, too. Rumor has it Sinatra has a piece of the action. Most people don't know that President John Kennedy, when he was a Senator, was an occasional guest of Sinatra right here at the Sands."

As the cab made a turn, the driver continued, "Here's the Desert Inn, Wilbur Clark's place. The money came from the old Cincinnati-Cleveland families." As they approached the Flamingo, traffic crawled to an almost stand still. Sitting in a traffic jam on Las Vegas Boulevard, the driver continued spewing his knowledge of the Vegas. "Here's another bit of information most people don't know - - the Las Vegas Strip is actually in Paradise, Nevada. They formed Paradise as an unincorporated town back in December, 1950, to avoid being annexed by Las Vegas.

Las Vegas Mayor Ernie Cragin was looking to fund an ambitious building agenda and pay down the city's rising debt. Cragin, sought to expand the city's tax base by annexing the Las Vegas Strip. A group of casino executives, led by Gus Greenbaum of the Flamingo would have none of that. Gus lobbied the county commissioners for township status to prevent the city from annexing the land without the commission's approval. Cragin was mad as hell that he lost all of that revenue."

"The story goes that the site where the Flamingo was built was owned by one of Las Vegas' first settlers, Charles 'Pops' Squires. He purchased the forty acre tract paying $8.75 an acre for the land. In 1944, Margaret Folsom paid Squires $7,500 for the tract. She later sold it to Billy Wilkerson, owner of the Hollywood Reporter."

Val was fascinated with the history lesson, but started to get suspicious. "Hey, how does a cabbie know so much about the details of the Flamingo and Las Vegas?"

Without hesitation, the cabbie snarled, "Hey lady, I'm writing a book about this town. I make it my business to know. You think I want to be a cabbie the rest of my life? Hell, maybe they'll make a movie from the book or something. Speaking of movies, they filmed *Ocean's Eleven* at the Sands and Elvis Presley and Ann Margret filmed *Viva Las Vegas* there in '64, I think."

"Really?" was all Val could say wondering about this dude.

The cabbie looked in the rearview mirror and continued his lecture. "Although Bugsy was thought to have been a genius by building a luxury hotel on the Vegas Strip, it was actually Billy Wilkerson's idea. In '45, he planned to build a hotel with luxurious rooms, a spa, health club, showroom, golf course, an upscale restaurant and nightclub. Wilkerson, however, ran into financial problems almost at once, finding himself $400,000 short and searching for new capital.

"Siegel purchased The El Cortez on Fremont Street for $600,000 and later sold it for a $166,000 profit at the same time that Wilkerson ran out of money. They were a match made in heaven. Siegel used his profits from the sale of the El Cortez to persuade Wilkerson to accept new partners. Siegel convinced Moe Sedway, Gus Greenbaum, and Meyer Lansky to invest $6 million into the new property. Wilkerson kept a one-third ownership stake and operating control.

"Siegel, being the shyster that he was, sold duplicate shares of the Flamingo to his friends and business associates. Siegel didn't care that he sold more than 200% interest in the joint just as long as the money kept pouring into the project.

"The Flamingo Hotel & Casino finally opened at a total cost of $6 million on December 26, 1946. The Flamingo, had a giant pink neon sign and replicas of pink flamingos on the lawn, and was touted as the world's most luxurious hotel. The one-hundred – plus room property was built seven miles from downtown Las Vegas. Bugsy wanted to have a place for his Hollywood friends, such as George Raft. Did you know he named this joint after his girlfriend, Virginia Hill? Her nickname was the Flamingo—a nickname some Mexicans gave her due to her long, skinny legs and flaming red hair. Heard she was one sexy dame who loved to drink, screw, and gamble."

Val did not say a word, but the sick feeling continued to nauseate her as she listened to the cab driver ramble on. As they approached the taxi stand at the Flamingo's entrance, the driver asked, "Did you know some guy named Kerkorian just purchased this place?" Val was thankful when they finally arrived at the Flamingo's taxi stand and she got out of the car.

As they made their way through the casino, the dice bounced on the green felt craps tables and rolled against the backstop, with the stickman calling out "seven, front line winner," and the riffle of cards being shuffled at the blackjack tables was like soft rain falling on a tin roof. The metallic sound of coins dropping into the trays from the one-armed bandits could be heard in chorus with bells and jingles as the roulette ball danced in and out of the slots on the moving wheel.

Without being distracted by the sights and sounds of the

casino, Val and Artimis found their way to the main bar.

"Hey bartender, you recognize this card?" Val asked, showing him the Queen of Hearts.

The bartender wiping down a glass with a linen towel looked at the card, "Nope, but Mickey, who has been here since the place opened, may know. He's on the floor someplace right now. Ask the front desk to page him for you."

Val, now in a more cheerful mood, was encouraged and said, "Thanks."

Val and Artimis headed towards the front desk and approached the clerk. "Can you page Mickey for us?" Val politely asked the clerk.

"Mickey who? Mickey Mouse?" retorted the desk clerk.

Artimis, in a swift inward motion, grabbed the desk clerk by the throat with his right hand before Val could say a word. "Listen smart ass - - are you gonna page Mickey for us or do I need to give you a knuckle sandwich?"

The clerk, his eyes bulging as his face turned bright red, nodded affirmatively and, as Artimis released his grip, quickly picked up the phone, dialed and said, "A guy and gal are up front asking to see you. No, no I don't know who they are or what they want."

The voice on the other end of the line asked, "What does the girl look like?"

The clerk described Val as she looked at him quizzically. The clerk then said, "Yes, I'll tell them to wait here for you," and hung up.

Sheepishly, the clerk asked Artimis and Val to wait at the front counter and that Mickey would be out shortly.

Artimis begrudgingly said, "Thank you." He and Val backed away slightly from the front counter to wait for Mickey.

Within a few minutes, Mickey approached Val and Artimis with a suspicious look. When he was close enough to see them without squinting, he said out loud, "I know you. I don't want to know you. I know you." Shaking his head as if indicating "no," Val and Artimis overheard him say, "I really don't want to know you."

Before Mickey had an opportunity to introduce himself, Val shoved the Queen of Hearts card in his face and asked, "Do you know what this means?"

Mickey did not flinch like Val expected, but calmly looked at the card and asked, "What else you got, toots?"

Val looked puzzled as she extended the envelope toward Mickey, and said, "This letter, these cards, photos, and this envelope." She handed Mickey the envelope saying nothing about the cash.

Mickey took it from Val and gave it a quick once over. A slight smile came across his face as he handed everything back to Val. "Kid, do yourself a favor. What you want ain't here. Go back to LA and forget you ever saw this stuff. If what you're looking for was here, you wouldn't be." Mickey turned to start to walk away thinking to himself, "Great, just peachy, Kirk Kerkorian purchased the Flamingo, hired Sahara Hotels Vice President Alex Shoofey as President Shaw gets himself eliminated, and now she shows up."

Val's face became red as the veins in her neck bulged out and she screamed out in a voice that reminded Mickey of his past, "You son of a bitch; how do you know I'm from LA? You know who I am, and who my parents were. What the fuck should I be looking for? Tell me, I want to know now!"

Mickey was not fazed with Val's rant. He had heard the yelling and screaming between Ben and Virginia so many times before that he became accustomed to it, despite it being more than twenty years ago. Mickey turned around and stared directly at Val, then, with a sigh and shrug of his shoulders, said, "Look at the Queen of Clubs. Once you figure out the message, then we will talk some more. If you can't figure it out - - well, there is nothing else to discuss. Capiche?" Mickey turned away again. This time he looked back and made a departing comment, "Nice tattoo."

Val was puzzled, glared at him, wondering how the hell he knew about her birthmark when she never mentioned it and it could not be seen. She turned to Artimis, "Hey, how did he know I was from L.A.? And how does he know about my birthmark?"

Artimis looked perplexed and tired. Not wanting to get into another discussion with Val, he simply said, "Beats the heck out of me. But the clue on the Queen of Hearts did say help will be waiting in a mysterious way. That guy sure was mysterious."

Val looked disheveled and worn out. Barely above a whisper had she said, "More creepy than mysterious?"

"Hey Val it's been a long day. Can we find a place to crash for the night and start tomorrow morning? I'm really beat." Artimis's long, sandy brown hair was shabby and his appearance was scruffy at best from not shaving and the long, hot Vegas sun was taking its toll on him. Val looked as rundown as Artimis and said, "Sure, let's get a room here for tonight - double beds."

Artimis was thinking to himself as they approached the registration deck, "Hmm, double beds . . . that's a better start than separate rooms."

Chapter 8

Peter Atwood, an FBI agent in his late twenties, was assigned to investigate the incident at the MGM studio. Atwood, standing 5'8", was shorter than most FBI agents, had short dark hair, and spoke softly but with authority. Wearing the standard FBI apparel, a white shirt, solid navy blue tie and black suit with polished shoes, he remained calm and collective at the crime scene which was roped off with yellow police tape.

Crossing under the tape, he spoke to detective Keith Malone of the Beverly Hills police department. Atwood wanted answers. "So what do we have here, detective?"

Detective Malone was a 6' tall Irishman with a slender build, short blond hair, a pug nose, and deep blue eyes. His twenty years on the police force left him with a sullen temperament. Like agent Atwood, Malone was clean shaven. His face was radiant, so much so that Hollywood stars envied his flawless skin. Malone's navy blue pin-striped suit was perfectly pressed as was his white shirt. He wore a solid dark burgundy tie that would have looked almost black if it weren't for the bright L.A. sun.

Malone, in a condescending manner, replied, "The guard at the security gate said the victim in the car gave his name as Sam Shaw. A business card was found in the blast area indicating Shaw was an attorney from Chicago. The Lincoln was a rental. We confirmed Shaw worked for the law firm Thornton, Mender and Bigelow. His office will not provide us with any details of the purpose of his trip to L.A. They're citing client privilege and confidentiality, although, in my opinion, I don't believe they have any clue why he was here in LA According to his secretary, a Miss Sheila White, she booked him a late night flight at the last moment, and he did not provide her with any other details. He was booked on the 4 p.m. flight back to Chicago yesterday. The office peppered with gun fire belongs to Artimis Sylver and his assistant Valentina Benjamin. Both work in special effects for the studio. No one has seen them since the explosion and gunfire. Our cursory inspection of the office did not indicate anyone was injured by the gunfire - no blood."

Atwood, though impressed with the details of Malone's, report was growing impatient because he was not being given what he considered more pertinent and relevant information. He pressed the issue with Malone, and asked, "Do we know who was doing the shooting?"

"No sir. The officers interviewing witnesses have not even had a description of the gunman as yet. According to witness accounts, it seems everyone was preoccupied with the explosion." Malone who was not happy that the FBI was even brought into this case then asked, "Sir, why is the FBI involved in this case so soon? We've barely have had an opportunity to do any investigation."

Atwood raised an eye brow. Without hesitation and without showing any sign of indignation. He curtly replied, "Well, Detective Malone, interstate murders always concern the FBI, especially when they involve a high-profile Chicago lawyer."

Malone pressed Atwood and asked, "Yes, but how did you know the victim was a high profile attorney from Chicago when I just told you this information?"

Atwood said, "The FBI received an anonymous tip just after the explosion. The tipster provided information that the victim was attorney Sam Shaw from Chicago and that this might be mob related. Headquarters assigned me to the case to investigate."

Atwood followed up, "Anything else on your mind detective?"

Malone shook his head and said, "No, sir."

Agent Atwood continued his conversation with Malone, "What I want to know is who was doing the shooting; who they were shooting at, why they were shooting at them, and what the connection is between Shaw and the people in this building?"

Atwood's voice was cool and soothing, almost mesmerizing Detective Malone who remained unruffled and composed. "Now, Detective, please get me a list of all visitors to the back lot this morning and as much information on Ms. Benjamin and Mr. Sylver as you can. And get a search warrant for this office."

"Yes, sir," Malone answered.

As Detective Malone departed, Atwood looked at the bullet holes on the outside wall of Artimis and Val's office building. Taking out a pair of tweezers from his pocket, he carefully removed a slug from the wall and gently placed it into a plastic evidence bag. Handing it to another agent, Atwood said, "Have ballistics run this for us."

Peering through the open doorway, he saw nothing out of the ordinary. Atwood backed away from the wall to study it further. He calculated that whoever it was that fired the shots intentionally missed the doorway.

Walking over to a rookie police officer stationed outside the door he asked, "What happened to the occupants of this office?"

The young police officer was looking down at his note pad as agent Atwood addressed him. He didn't look up at Atwood. The rookie officer thought Atwood was just another reporter and said, in a defiant voice, "Who the hell are you and what's it to you?" Atwood calmly pulled out his FBI badge and said in a serene voice with a broad smile on his face, "FBI Agent Atwood. And you are?"

The police officer looked up at Atwood and glanced at his badge. "Officer Dirkens, sir. My apologies." Dirkens sheepishly continued, "Unknown, sir. The security guard at the rear gate said he saw Artimis Sylver and Valentina Benjamin leave the parking lot immediately after the explosion and firing of shots had ended. According to the guard, they didn't seem to have much interest in all the commotion."

"Probably because they are part of this mess," Atwood murmured to himself as he turned to leave.

As Atwood was returning to his car, another police officer approached him and called out, "Sir, wait a moment. The station operator received a call from a person who said they have information about this case."

Atwood went over to the patrol officer and inquired as to the message. The officer said, "Our office just got a call from a Mickey Cohen in Las Vegas. He said he had some information about this situation that may interest you." The officer then handed Atwood a piece of paper and said, "Here is the number to call him."

Atwood took the paper from the officer and thought to himself, "What the heck does Cohen have to do with this?"

Atwood went back to talk with Detective Malone. "Detective, did any of your people try to contact Ms. Benjamin or Mr. Sylver at their residences?"

Malone did not express how annoyed he was with Atwood's question. Instead, with a monotone voice he answered, "Officers went to both residences. No one was home at either residence." Malone anticipated Atwood's next question and said, "We have officers trying to track them down. As soon as we hear anything we'll let you know."

Atwood left the scene wondering what Mickey Cohen might have to say.

Chapter 9

The last thing Artimis remembered before the telephone rang was Val bending over him in bed, kissing him, and saying, "You shouldn't sleep on my side of the bed, my love. It's bad for your health. Roll over." Obediently, he rolled over and as the door clicked shut he was fast asleep again.

The phone rang again in the dark room and kept on ringing. Artimis cursed, his head pounding, as he reached for the phone. A voice said, "Sorry to disturb you, sir. This is the front desk. We were instructed to wake you at noon." "Now what is she up to," Artimis thought? All the beauty, heat of the moment, and excitement of their passionate lovemaking from the previous night were pushed away. Reality set in. As he turned on the lights, Artimis was thinking, "was it a dream, or had Val and he actually made love?" He opened the curtains just slightly to let in the daylight. Shaking his head to clear it he stepped into the shower, not certain of what had happened the night before.

There was a knock on the door before the key opened it. "'Bout time you woke up," Val said as she stepped into the room and pulled the curtains wide open. The fiery glow of the neon lights no longer lit up the sky as the sun shown vibrantly over the strip. "You ready to continue this fishing expedition?" she said.

Artimis toweled himself dry, wrapped it around his waist and said, "Right after we have breakfast. But first I need to get dressed." Eventually he found his clothes. He removed the towel and slid on his faded blue jeans and a tie dye tee shirt. Artimis continued cautiously with his next question, "Val did something happen between us last night?"

Val was gazing out the window. She was wearing bell bottom jeans and a white button peasant blouse. Even without make-up, she was radiant. "What exactly do you mean?" she quipped. Artimis, not knowing if she was toying with him or was dead serious, asked more to the point, "Did we make love last night?"

Val blushed at the question, "Hell no! What gave you that idea?"

Artimis, not really paying attention to what Val was saying repeated, "Val, I need to know about last night. Did we make love?"

Val giggled and responded, "You wish; only in your dreams."

Artimis shook his head in disbelief and said, "Man that was some dream. I don't remember anything except waking up this morning when the phone rang."

Val, with a big smile on her face, almost burst out into laughter and said, "That's because I put a sleeping pill in your drink last night. You were getting too many ideas about us 'sleeping' together."

Artimis, in a humorless tone, responded, "You drugged me?"

Val, still smiling, said, "Yes, yes I did - - it was for your own safety. I told you, it's dangerous for you to be in my bed let alone on my side of the bed." The conversation ended with nothing else said on the subject.

Val watched Artimis as he finished brushing and drying his hair. "You ready for lunch. It's already afternoon," she said as she made her way to the door.

They were about to leave the room when the phone rang again. Artimis answered and spoke for a few minutes before hanging up. "It was Mickey calling to make sure you were alright. He said he had a suspicious feeling about your safety. He also wanted to let you know he changed the names we registered under to ensure we don't have any uninvited guests." Smiling, he continued, "We are now Mr. and Mrs. John Smith. Apparently, Mickey has friends in high places and made some inquiries about your package. Come on, let's get some food before we start back on our quest."

They entered the Flamingo's hotel lobby, with the opulent marble floor, high ceiling, and crystal chandeliers hanging overhead, and headed for the café bearing Bugsy's name. Artimis noticed a man in dark sunglasses staring straight at Val as they followed the hostess to their seats. Petite and sporting a near perfect figure, Val seldom failed to attract the male eye. She looked effervescent even with her hair pulled back.

As they looked over the menu, Artimis glanced up and spotted the man in the sunglasses who had eyed Val earlier. He looked directly at him from across several other tables. Without saying a word, Artimis then slowly glanced around the restaurant to see who else might be watching. As he casually surveyed the crowd, Artimis noticed a thin man with long, blond hair tied back in a ponytail, watching them and trying to look inconspicuous by reading a newspaper. Artimis had a feeling that others may also be watching.

"You look paranoid," Val said as she broke Artimis' concentration. Artimis relaxed, retuned his focus back to the menu and said, "I am. We're being watched."

Artimis lowered his menu and looked at Val solemnly, "Seriously."

Val put her menu down on the table and said, "Well I'm hungry, and I'm going to eat first before our guests decide to make a move."

Without saying much else, the two ordered as the waitress brought two cups of coffee to their table. Artimis ordered eggs over easy with bacon, an English muffin, and a side of hash browns. Val ordered the fruit and melon plate. They ate their meal without much conversation.

As they finished their meals, Artimis told Val to act as if she was making her way to the ladies room, and he would follow her later to meet at the valet.

The café's waitress appeared and asked if they wanted more coffee and possibly desert. Val started to shake her head, but Artimis spoke up, "Yes, please."

"I don't want any more coffee or desert, especially now." She glared at Artimis.

He grinned and said, "Change in plans. Desert is for our friends, to buy us some time. Make a show that you need to use the ladies room then go get a taxi. I'll meet you outside."

Val smiled at Artimis and winked at him. She slowly rose, and asked a nearby busboy for directions to the ladies room. Artimis watched and observed the man with the long ponytail straighten and place his hands on the table as if to get up as Val headed towards the restrooms, but relaxed when the waitress appeared with a piece of pie and poured more coffee. Artimis covertly slipped a one hundred dollar bill on the table and then stuck a fork into the pie. After taking a few bites and sipping some more coffee, Artimis slipped away from the table when the opportunity arose as the man with the ponytail was distracted by a cute keno girl. Artimis headed swiftly towards the lobby.

Looking over his shoulder, Artimis noticed the man with the sunglasses walking next to the man with the ponytail, and another man hurriedly following behind. Without hesitation, Artimis walked out the front door and saw Val waiting in her Mustang. He jumped into the passenger seat and told her to go across the street to Caesars Palace.

Chapter 10

Caesars Palace commanded an imposing view from the Strip. White polished marble sculptures, larger than life, imposed their glorious figures from days long past along the walkway to the casino entrance. The monuments brought Rome's celebrated past to life in the Vegas desert oasis. A high wall of shrubs encircled the stone figures giving them a more impressive presence. The eyes of locals and tourists alike gazed upon them with awe.

Val, uncertain of what Artimis had in mind, pulled her red convertible Mustang into the Caesars' parking lot across from the Flamingo.

As Artimis walked around the car and slipped into the driver's seat, he looked at Val with a puzzled expression. "Hey, how did you get your car from L.A. to Vegas?"

Val, finishing the slide over to the passenger side said, "My dad drove it in this morning. According to his story, he received a strange phone call last night requesting him to deliver the car to the Flamingo. He called me while you were still asleep. I called Ernie and asked him what was going on. Ernie said he got a call to make sure the car was delivered to my parent's home last night. That's all I know."

Artimis, looking more confused than ever, asked, "Where's your dad now?"

Val nonchalantly replied, "Probably home by now. I dropped him at the airport before I came back to our room to get you." As Artimis put the car into gear and began to move forward, he asked, "By the way, before Ernie brought the car back to your parents' home, did he get a chance to add some of those special features from the James Bond movie *Goldfinger* that I mentioned?"

Val said, "Yes, he did. Ernie was very inquisitive, but I told him you would make it worth his while if he kept this under wraps." Val smiled as she watched Artimis' expression turn from smugness to frantic, "What?" she asked.

Artimis said, "I'm worried what Ernie's going to want for his silence."

As Artimis drove through Caesar's long driveway, he stopped when they reached Las Vegas Boulevard. Without hesitating, Artimis shifted through the gears and was on Las Vegas Boulevard within seconds. Turning left out of Caesar's parking lot, Artimis had just passed the Imperial Palace with its famous car collection, Harrah's Holiday Inn with its riverboat wheel, and Casino Royale's Nob Hill when he noticed a black Lincoln Continental a few cars behind them. Unable to see the driver or other passengers in the Lincoln, Artimis decided to test to see if, in fact, they were being followed.

Making a quick right onto Spring Mountain Road and then another left onto Koval, Artimis saw the black Lincoln gaining ground and coming up fast behind them.

Artimis rapidly shifted through the gears as he told Val, "Hang on. We've got company."

With its 385 horsepower and 460 cubic inch V-8, the Lincoln easily kept up with the Mustang's speed. It did not, however, have the same maneuvering capability.

As the Lincoln began to gain ground, Artimis put the Mustang into fourth gear and floored it. Heading towards the desert, Val, curious to see what Ernie had added to her car, opened the glove compartment. Two M1911 pistols fell out onto the floorboard in front of her..

"I asked Ernie to borrow them from the set. They're props, but instead of shooting blanks I asked him to put live ammo in the magazine," Artimis said.

"Live ammo! Are you out of your mind? You want me to shoot at them?" Val screamed at Artimis. He sarcastically yelled back, "No, I want you to just wave it at them. What do you think? Do you even know how to shoot a gun?"

"Yes I do!" Val said. "I had to learn about weapons for one of our films."

The M1911 was a single-action, semi-automatic, magazine-fed, and recoil-operated handgun. Designed by John M. Browning, the M1911 was chambered for .45 ACP cartridges.

"Let's see about this other stuff, Val said, looking at a control panel with several switches.

"Don't touch any of those switches unless Ernie told you what they do," Artimis snarled at her.

She just looked at him with a worried look not knowing what to say or what to expect. Her only thought was that if Ernie screwed up, they were going to die.

Approximately twenty miles out of town and well into the desert, the Black Lincoln was right behind the Mustang. Despite Artimis driving the Mustang at speeds over one-hundred miles per hour, the Lincoln had no problem keeping up with them. The passenger in the Lincoln emerged through the window and began shooting at Val and Artimis. Bullets riddled Val's Mustang. The back vinyl window was shredded by several bullets. Artimis, driving in a zigzag pattern to avoid being hit, yelled at Val, "Do something - hit one of the switches."

Val's fingers quickly moved across the control panel, and she pushed the blue switch forward and smoke poured out of the trunk. The smoke screen was effective for only a few seconds but successfully blinded the driver of the Lincoln.

"Hit another switch now," Artimis called out.

Quickly and without hesitation, Val moved the green switch forward. This time nails and barbs were dropped on the pavement behind them. The Lincoln was unable to swerve in time to avoid hitting the nails and the front driver side wheel blew out. Unable to handle the vehicle at such a high speed, the driver lost control, and the Lincoln flipped over twice, before coming to a screeching halt as metal sparks flew across the road and into the desert.

Both the driver and the passenger got out of the car staggering to their feet. The driver had a gash on his forehead, and blood oozed out across his nose and down his cheek. The other man appeared unhurt, just dazed.

Without hesitation, Artimis hit the brakes. He turned the steering wheel hard to the left, made a quick u-turn and headed back towards the Lincoln.

Still stunned, the driver and passenger did not realize they were dead to rites that Val and Artimis were staring at them with their guns drawn and pointed at them. "Hands up," yelled Artimis.

With his hands in the air, the driver of the Lincoln, was wiping blood from his face and said in a defiant voice, "We ain't saying anything to you."

Val did not hesitate and said, "Either you start talking or you die right here. Your choice; what's it going to be?"

"Fuck you bitch," yelled the driver of the Lincoln.

Without hesitating, much like her biological father, Bugsy, Val fired the gun, putting a bullet in the driver's forehead. Artimis looked at Val surprised, stunned, and a bit frightened. The driver also had a stunned expression as his body crumpled to the ground. Blood started to ooze from the bullet hole in his head to mix with the blood already flowing from the gash.

Val looked at the next man and said, "You're next unless I get some answers."

As Artimis looked at the dead man lying on the road, a vision of Bugsy Siegel flashed before his eyes. Artimis had a fleeting thought that maybe Val was Bugsy reincarnated.

Speaking with a heavy Italian accent, the passenger from the Lincoln yelled back, "Okay, okay lady, what do ya want to know?"

Val, with her left arm wiped the sweat off her brow. The desert sun beat down on them with no mercy. Val kept her pistol pointed at the man's head the entire time, never taking her eyes off him. "What's your name?" she asked.

"Jerry."

Val then asked, "Okay Jerry, why are you following us?"

Jerry was sweating profusely through his black polo shirt. The beads of sweat dripped from his face and started to form a small puddle at his feet, "My boss says you got something of his and that he wants it returned."

Artimis remained quiet during the entire time Val questioned Jerry. He, too, was feeling the effects of the scorching sun burning down on him.

Val continued her questioning, "What? What does he want?"

Jerry, still standing with his hands held in the air asked, "Hey, lady, can I at least put my hands down? It's fuckin hot out here." Val nodded in the affirmative. Jerry, with a slight sigh of relief lowered his hands to his side.

He glanced at Artimis, who still had his gun trained on him and continued, "The contents of that package you got the other day - something about a deed to the El Rancho Casino. That's all I know lady. We were just told to get the fuckin' envelope from you."

Val squinted to keep the sun from her eyes and asked, "Do you know who the hell I am?"

Jerry smiled. He had an amused look on his face, "Yeah - - you're Bugsy's and that fuckin' whore bitch Virginia Hill's kid."

Val fired her gun. The bullet whizzed past Jerry's left ear. Jerry yelled, "What the fuck you doin', lady?"

Artimis interrupted, "I don't think she liked what you said about her parents. Besides, she's got her father's temper, if you know what I mean."

Val thought to herself 'that should wipe the grin off the bastard's face.' She also thought, 'does everyone know who I am but me?' She then said to Jerry, "You'd better watch your tongue, or the next time I won't miss." Jerry apologized with some sincerity, but Val was not buying it.

Val asked him, "Who's your boss?"

Jerry was no longer smiling. The grin disappeared from his face. He knew that anything he divulged to Val would get back to Jordan Hamilton. Jerry's dark brown eyes were sullen as he thought long and hard before answering, "Jordan Hamilton."

Val waved the gun, still pointed at Jerry, in an up and down motion, yelling at him, "Who the hell is Jordan Hamilton?"

Jerry knew he had already said too much. Still he responded, "He's a Chicago businessman connected with the casinos here in Vegas."

Artimis lowered his weapon and joined the conversation, "Where is Mr. Hamilton now?"

Jerry directed his attention to Artimis. With a look of disdain, he quietly answered, "Probably back in Chicago - how should I know. The guy with all the information is lying there dead."

Val moved a few steps away from Jerry and lowered her gun. In a businesslike tone she asked, "How do I contact Mr. Hamilton?"

Jerry sighed with relief seeing that both Artimis and Val were not pointing guns in his face and said, "Lady, you don't contact him. He contacts you."

Artimis interrupted Val's interrogation, "What now?" he asked.

Val, with a menacing, maniacal grin, pointed her gun at Jerry and said, "You got anything in the trunk you can use to dig with?"

"What?" retorted Jerry, with a bewildered and astonished look on his face. Val raised her weapon again and repeated, "I asked you if you have anything to dig with. Don't make me ask again."

Jerry, now feeling apprehensive about his situation, hastily responded, "A shovel. We were told to bury you two out here."

"Open the trunk," Val instructed Jerry. Without another word, Jerry opened the trunk, revealing, not one, but two shovels, and array of other items.

Val instructed Jerry, "Good. Start digging a hole, because I want you to fill it with your friend. It's either that, or I shoot you too."

As Jerry started digging, Val rummaged through the contents of the trunk. Artimis kept a watchful eye on Jerry, his gun pointed at him the entire time.

Val called out to Jerry as he continued to dig the hole, "You two must be fuckin' idiots. Did you really think I would keep that envelope with me?"

Approximately an hour and a half later, Jerry was about to toss the dead man's body, into the hole, when Val said, "Wait. Before you dump him, cut off his pinky finger, the one with the ring on it. Use this."

Val tossed Jerry a piece of metal from the smashed Lincoln. He did as he was told.

Puzzled, Artimis looked at Val and asked, "Why the hell do you want this son of a bitch's pinky finger? If you wanted the ring you could just have had Jerry remove it."

Val, in an agitated and anxious voice, said, "A small gift for Mr. Hamilton. I'm sure he'll recognize the ring and know we mean business. The finger is just a subtle warning." Jerry then sliced off the dead man's finger. Val, watching him complete the barbaric act, said in an authoritative voice, "Now put it in this rag and bury your friend."

Jerry followed Val's orders and buried the man without any comment.

"What are we going to do with him?" Artimis asked. He was looking at Jerry who was sweating profusely, his clothing drenched in perspiration.

Jerry, his head hung low from exerting himself, did not notice Val grab the second shovel and whack him in the head, knocking him out cold. Val tossed a piece of rope towards Artimis, "Here's some rope I found in the trunk. Tie him up and put him in the back seat. We'll drop him off at Mickey's. He can deal with Jerry."

Val fired a shot at the gas tank of the Lincoln. A spark flashed as the car caught fire. As the car burned and smoke began to fill the desert sky, Val said to Artimis, "Let's go before the cops show up."

Artimis looked at Val and said, "Val you're starting to scare me."

Val walked at a brisk pace toward her car and said, "Too bad! I'm pissed. Look what they did to my car." The Mustang was riddled with bullet holes. The body of the car looked like craters on the moon.

Artimis wanting to add some levity to the situation said, "Come on, let's go. I'm sure Mickey knows of a body shop to get it fixed."

As they drove up to the main entrance of the Flamingo, Val and Artimis were greeted outside by a valet. The valet looked at the holes that riddled the Mustang, "Are those bullet holes?" he asked.

Artimis, hot and sweaty from spending too much time in the desert sun, said, "Souvenirs from some business associates."

The valet stared in fascination at the holes and asked, "They tried to kill you? When did this happen?"

Artimis answered impassively as he moved the front seat forward to let Jerry exit the car, "Just about an hour ago." Val exited the car from the passenger side and asked with a smile, "Know of a good body shop?" Jerry was sweating and perspiring profusely as he exited the Mustang. He wobbled groggily and didn't say a word as Artimis handed the keys to the valet. They walked into the lobby of the casino looking like they had been through the ringer. The valet stood motionless still unsure of what to do or say at the sight of the bullet riddled car.

Finally, he collected his wits and got into the Mustang. Instead of parking the car, he drove away, presumably to bring it to the body shop.

Chapter 11

Martha answered the door before the doorbell rang a second time. Wearing an apron and wiping her hands as she opened the door, a man was standing in front of her with a big smile on his face. Martha did not notice the sinister manner of the smile as her focus was on the gun being held at his waist level, and pointed directly at her.

From the kitchen area, Stewart yelled out, "Who's at the door, dear?"

Martha, still in shock from having a gun pointed at her was unable to reply.

"May I come in?" asked the man.

Martha motioned for him to enter the house. As the man entered, he put the gun away. As he did so, Stewart entered the living room to see Jordan Hamilton remove his hat.

"Good afternoon, folks," Jordan said to the couple. "My apologies, sorry to barge in this way, but your daughter has something in her possession that I want."

"What could Val possibly have that you would want?" asked Martha, obviously rattled by the intrusion of Hamilton.

"A deed to some property," he replied calmly. "So until your daughter returns it to me, I will be your house guest."

Stewart looked at Hamilton. Hamilton was wearing an expensive, tailored, navy blue, pinstriped business suit, a powder blue shirt, and a dark blue tie. His silver-gray hair was neatly trimmed and his fingernails were perfectly manicured. Stewart, undaunted by Hamilton's demeanor and high profile appearance, said, "Like hell you will. You get out of this house now or I'm calling the cops."

Jordan did not say a word. He simply pulled out his gun, pointed it at Stewart and motioned for Martha and him to head towards the kitchen. With a defeated look, Stewart took Martha's hand and walked with him.

A few hours passed before the telephone rang. Hamilton, who had removed his suit jacket and hung it on the back of a kitchen chair, told Martha to answer it. "Hello," Martha said in a quivering voice.

Val, who was on the other end of the line asked, "Mom, are you alright?"

Martha looked deep into Hamilton's mesmerizing light brown eyes and replied in a calmer voice, "Yes, dear." Hamilton grabbed the phone from Martha and said, "Val, so nice to hear your voice."

Val, shocked by the interruption of an unfamiliar voice, retorted, "Who the hell is this?"

"Jordan Hamilton."

Val's reaction was hostile as she said, "You motherfucker son-of-a-bitch!" What do you want and why are you trying to kill me?"

Hamilton said, "I believe you have in your possession the deed to the El Rancho Hotel and Casino, and some other pertinent documents. I want them!"

Val, who was starting to take on the personality of Bugsy, was fuming. Unknown to Hamilton, Artimis was watching Val as she spoke. Artimis could tell that something was definitely wrong but remained silent. Val with an edge to her tone asked, "What makes you so certain I have the deed?"

Hamilton had kept his composure and with a frigid voice answered, "Because Virginia had it and I think it was in that envelope you received from attorney Shaw."

Val trying to buy some time to think of her next move said, "Let me call you back in five minutes. I need to look at what I have with me."

Hamilton said, "Five minutes" as he hung up the phone.

Turning to Martha and Stewart, he grinned and said, "Hopefully I won't be your house guest much longer.

Val, upon ending her conversation with Hamilton, immediately called Mickey. She told Mickey what was happening at her parents' house and that her parents were being threatened and held hostage by Hamilton. Mickey assured Val her parents would not be harmed and that he would take care of the matter. Val, confident that Mickey would keep her parents safe, hung-up the phone with him and then filled Artimis in on what was going on.

Mickey, after talking to Val, called the Benjamin's residence to speak to Jordan Hamilton. Hamilton, who was not aware that Cohen was now directly mixed up in the business, answered the phone. Mickey, immediately upon hearing Jordan's voice, said, "Jordan, Mickey Cohen. Val doesn't have the deed. I saw the contents of the envelope. I'm not saying that she couldn't get the deed. I'm just saying she doesn't have it yet. Leave her parents out of this, and we can talk. Anything happens to them and you know what will happen."

Hamilton's faced stiffened as he responded, "Mickey, you double-cross me, and I'll make certain every one of them is dead. You got that?" Hamilton's tone was alarming to Martha and Stewart.

Stewart held Martha's hand and tried to assure her that everything would be okay.

Hamilton handed the phone back to Martha, turned and walked out the front door without saying a word to her or Stewart.

Martha, took the phone, hung it up, and looked at Stewart, puzzled, but that look also had a sigh of relief. They hugged each other.

Stewart said, "I'm not so certain this is the end of it."

Martha, with tears streaming down her face, was still hugging Stewart and said, "I hope you're wrong."

About twenty minutes after Hamilton left the Benjamin residence, Val called to make certain her parents were all right. Martha, hearing Val on the other end of the phone line said, "Val, what's going on?"

Val, not answering her mother's question asked, "Mom, are you okay?"

Martha who was sipping a glass of chardonnay to calm herself down after the ordeal with Hamilton answered, "Yes, dear, that other man left our home about twenty minutes ago. Whatever your friend said to him must have satisfied him because he walked out the front door without saying a word."

Val with an air of confidence, said, "Mom, it's complicated. I'll explain everything to you and dad soon. In the meantime, Artimis and I have some unfinished business here in Vegas. I'll call you later."

As Val hung up, Martha started to speak, but heard the dial

tone. She turned to Stewart who had been listening to Martha's end of the conversation and crumpled into his arms, sobbing.

* * *

Mickey waited until the next morning to call Hamilton. It was a short drive from L.A. to Vegas. Hamilton was back in his suite at Caesar's. Mickey, in a calm, collective tone, not being unnerved by Hamilton, asked, "Did you get Val's message to keep your goons away from her?" He continued, "I just wanted to make certain you understood the message about the package delivered to your suite at Caesar's."

Mickey had Jerry deliver a small, white cardboard gift box to Jordan Hamilton, shortly after the ordeal in the desert, knowing Hamilton was staying at Caesar's Palace in Vegas.

After Jordan received the package from Mickey, he initially smirked and set the box on the desk in his suite without opening it. As he set the box down, he thought to himself, "Mickey has no idea who he's dealing with."

A few minutes after his guest left, Jordan decided to open the box. His henchmen were milling around the suite as a look of despair came across Jordan Hamilton's face. Not much could disturb Hamilton's cool demeanor, but he was aghast at what was inside the box.

Looking astonished, he realized that the ring finger inside the gift box belonged to his assistant, Tony Iannotti. The finger still had the ring given to him by Hamilton on it. A note enclosed with the finger said, "Back off."

Hamilton said to Mickey, "Yeah, I understood your message. I'm back in Vegas; let's meet where we can talk in private."

"Agreed," was all Mickey said as he hung up the phone.

Chapter 12

Back in his office, Agent Atwood was speaking to detective Malone about the studio incident. "So, Malone, do we have any answers yet?"

Malone responded, "No, sir. Still haven't located Artimis Sylver or Valentina Benjamin. An officer spoke to her landlord and roommate, but neither had much information. According to the landlord, Valentina and a man fitting the description of Sylver showed up shortly after a few men had ransacked her apartment. No report was filed with the police. The landlord thinks they are involved in some drug deal. An officer also spoke to Valentina's roommate, Miss Annette Gerrard. Miss Gerrard told the officer she had no idea of Valentina's whereabouts or about what was taken from their apartment. She did say that Valentina left a note that she and Artimis would be on a film shoot for a few weeks. "

Atwood rubbed his chin. His face was composed as he continued his conversation with Malone, "What do we know about Valentina Benjamin?"

Malone reported, "Not too much. I sent an agent to her parent's home to ask them if they knew the whereabouts of their daughter. The officer reported back that her parents, Stewart and Martha Benjamin, were not very cooperative. According to the officer, they didn't know where their daughter was, and if they did, they weren't saying."

Atwood was unhappy with the progress of the investigation. He could sense that the case was a low priority for the police because they felt it was a mob hit. Atwood told Malone, "Okay, get out of here and get me some answers." Malone left Atwood's office with a slight grin on his face.

Agent Atwood looked at the piece of paper with Mickey Cohen's telephone number on it. Picking up the telephone he dialed the number. After three rings a voice on the other end said, "Cohen here."

"Mickey Cohen?" inquired Atwood.

Mickey, in a low voice said, "Yeah, who's asking?"

"FBI Agent Atwood speaking, I understand you have some information for me about the MGM murder."

Mickey Cohen's face lit up with delight, "Ah, Agent Atwood. 'Bout time you decided to call me. Here's the deal. You back off your investigation, and I'll give you some answers now and the person responsible for Attorney Shaw's murder. I need you to keep the FBI and local cops out of this mess. Otherwise there will be more dead bodies."

Atwood already felt like he was being played by Malone and the LA Police Department so he considered for a second, and then said, "First you give me some information before I decide to back off. Who is Valentina Benjamin and how does she fit into this case?"

Mickey knew he had to give Atwood something to make him stand down, "Valentina Benjamin is the biological daughter of Benjamin 'Bugsy' Siegel and Virginia Hill. Virginia made arrangements just before Bugsy was killed to have Martha and Stewart Benjamin adopt Valentina."

Atwood was stunned at Mickey's disclosure and said in a harsh tone, "I didn't know Virginia and Bugsy had a child together. What kind of bullshit are you feeding me?"

Mickey had no reason to mislead Atwood and said, "Ain't no bullshit. Fact is, no one knew except Virginia's brother, Chick, the attorney who handled the paperwork, and me. They kept everything under wraps, waiting until she turned twenty-one. Shaw delivered an envelope to Valentina. The envelope was from Virginia. It's been in Thornton's law firm since 1952. No one knew the contents, not even Shaw. Thornton was told to deliver the package to Valentina after her 21st birthday. That's what started this mess. Someone in Thornton's office tipped someone else off about the delivery."

Atwood realized that Mickey was leveling with him and asked, "How does Artimis Sylver fit into this?"

Mickey answered, "From what my sources tell me, he's her boss at the studio. I gather he's interested in being more than just a boss. I'm not sure how he got involved, but he's with her now."

Atwood pressed Mickey and asked, "How did they know about Valentina being adopted if it was a secret?"

Mickey replied, "I haven't a clue. Someone must have let it slip. For all I know it could have been Chick when he was in prison. I really can't help you there."

Atwood, seizing an opportunity to find out where his two subjects may be hiding asked, "You know where they're at?"

Mickey said in a defiant voice, "Of course I do. They're here in Vegas where I can keep an eye on them. You can't come here, because there are other factions at work. Atwood, you really don't want any piece of this shit. I'm asking you nicely and telling you that you'd better stay away for now. I'll keep you posted as this thing plays out."

Atwood pondered the information Mickey had just given him. After a moment's pause, he said, "No promises. I'm warning you now that if you can't deliver, I'm going to charge you with impeding an investigation and obstruction of justice. Do you know who killed Shaw?"

Cohen responded, "Not certain yet, but I have some leads I'm following up. Chicago family members are involved. That's all I'm gonna tell you for now. And don't make any more idle threats about obstruction of justice. You know I don't give a fuck 'bout the law."

Atwood quickly asked, "One more thing, anything to do with drugs? One of our sources said it was a drug deal gone south."

Mickey chuckled. "Seriously? Not even close."

Atwood said, "Okay, we have a deal. You'd better not be fucking with me, Cohen."

The conversation ended with nothing further said.

Chapter 13

Artimis and Val were back in their room at the Flamingo. Val was looking at the Queen of Clubs, pacing back and forth across the floor.

Val read out loud the clue on the Queen of Clubs, from the Sands Casino:

> *"The Lady swinging on the Moon will guide your way."*
> *"Peter is his name I say. A Rat just the same. A*
> *present he has for you but only if you, can find the way."*

"What does this mean?" Val said to herself as she read the clue over and over.

"Can I see it?" asked Artimis extending his hand to take the card from Val. "Mickey said we had to figure out the clue on the Queen of Clubs before he would help us." Artimis was looking at the card and read the clue out loud to himself. As he examined what was written on the card, he asked Val, "What else is in the envelope?"

Val picked up the envelope and poured all of its contents on the bed. It only contained the four cards, the letter from Virginia, and several photographs. Val had already put the $30,000 in a safe place. The first photo was a picture of Mickey and Benjamin Siegel standing in front of the Flamingo. On the back of the photo was a scribbled note saying, "Grand re-opening, March, 1947 despite the hotel not being complete. This time is a lot different than the December 1946 opening." The neon sign on top of the casino's roof was a red elongated rectangle with a flamingo on the top and white letters spelling out FLAMINGO running down from just beneath the flamingo bird to the top of the roof. Standing approximately twenty feet in height, the sign was taller than the building itself. Just below the sign, Mickey and Bugsy were shown shaking hands pointing to the large sign.

The second photo was a picture of Frank Sinatra playing at a craps table with Dean Martin and Virginia standing between the two of them. It was a black and white photo and the background appeared almost black as if the craps table was in a dark cavern. Martin and Sinatra were dressed in tuxedos, and Virginia was wearing a classic evening gown.

The third photo was a picture of John F. Kennedy, Marilyn Monroe, and Virginia sitting at a bar booth in one of the casinos having drinks.

The fourth photo was a picture of Virginia and her brother, Chick, standing in front of The Sahara Casino.

The fifth photo was a postcard from the El Rancho Casino. Nothing was written on the back.

Artimis was looking at the clue on the Queen of Clubs and turned it over to the back side. Muttering out loud to himself he said, "Nothing on the back." He turned towards Val, "Let me see the Queen of Hearts." Val handed him the Queen of Hearts. Artimis turned it over to its back side. "Hey Val, the Queen of Hearts is from the Flamingo and the Queen of Clubs is from the Sands."

Val, unimpressed, said, "Yeah, so what?"

Artimis, in an excited voice, said, "Let me see the photos." Val handed Artimis the photos. "I think these photos might help solve the riddles. Look here at this photo," he said as he showed Val the photo of Mickey and Bugsy standing in front of the Flamingo. "I'll bet you anything this photo corresponds to the Queen of Hearts."

Val looked at the photo and the Queen of Hearts and said, "Okay, well that makes sense. The letter made solving the first riddle easy." "Which photo goes with the Queen of Clubs?" Val asked.

As he looked at the photo of Frank Sinatra, Virginia, and Dean Martin standing at the craps table he saw that the name Sands was written across the layout. "Hey Val, the Queen of Clubs card is from the Sands!"

Val said in a blasé voice, "Duh, I already told you that. Besides, the back of the card indicates that the Queen of Clubs is from the Sands. What's the big deal?"

Artimis elatedly pointed at the photo of Sinatra, Martin and Virginia standing at a craps table, "Look, look at the name on the craps table layout – it says Sands right here. See?"

Val looked at the photo. She then turned it over to see if anything was written on the back. She was disappointed seeing that the back of the photo was blank.

Quickly, she picked up the photo of John F. Kennedy, Marilyn Monroe, and Virginia sitting at the booth in one of the casinos having drinks. Gazing at the photo, she noticed a menu on the white table cloth in front of Virginia. The menu was from the Dunes. "Artimis, you're right. This photo has a menu from the Dunes in it. The Queen of Spades card was from the Dunes." Again turning the photo over, she was disappointed to see it, too, was blank. "At least now we can match the cards with the photos," Val said.

Artimis picked up the photo of Virginia and Chick standing in front of the Sahara and looked at the Queen of Diamonds card, which was from the Sahara Casino.

Val, seeing Artimis with the photo, asked, "Is there anything written on the back of the photo?"

Artimis looked at the back of the photo and replied, "No, it's blank. Why do you ask?"

Val looked at Artimis, a frown on her face, "Because the photo of Mickey and Bugsy has a note scribbled on the backside."

Artimis, still holding the photo of Virginia and Chick and the Queen of Diamonds card, looked at Val and asked, "Anything interesting?"

Val looked at the back of the photo from the Flamingo and said, "Not really. It just says, 'Grand re-opening, March, 1947, despite the hotel not being complete. This time is a lot different than the December 1946 opening'."

Artimis with a serious expression said, "This is starting to make sense. At least we know where to start looking."

Val, in an excited voice, said, "Let's check out the Sands since the card is from there. Maybe someone will know something."

Artimis, who always seemed to have an appetite, asked, "First, can we get some lunch? I'm hungry."

Val responded, "Always thinking about food, huh? We can get some lunch at the Sands. First, I want to put all of this in the safe deposit box at the front desk."

There, Val asked the clerk for a safe deposit box. It was customary for the larger casinos to provide safe deposit boxes for guests who did not want to leave valuables such as jewelry and cash in their rooms. Feeling better after placing the envelope and its contents in the box, Val realized she too, was hungry and was ready for lunch.

Val and Artimis were looking at the menu in the cafeteria at the Sands when Artimis looked up into the distance. He noticed an oil painting of a lady wearing a bright red, western-style dress, sitting on a moon near the cashier's station. After ordering their meals, Artimis got up from the table to get a closer look, and Val sighed, "Now where are you going?"

Artimis was focused and did not hear Val's question. Without answering, he walked closer to the painting to get a better look at it. He noticed a plate on the right hand side of the painting which read, "Donated by members of the Rat Pack." The painting was 30" x 40" with an ornate gold wood frame. The lady was wearing a red western-style dress with a blue top covering her breasts and cowboy boots. She sat on a crescent shaped moon. Her red hair was about shoulder length and was covered by a yellow witch's hat. She was holding a glass of beer in her left hand held up high as if making a toast. Around her in a circle was a background of a night sky with the stars shining bright. Next to the painting on the left hand side was another small plaque indicating the painting was originally done for Miller High Life. Val watched Artimis as he returned to the table. He had a broad grin on his face as if he just got laid and sat down.

Val waited a few seconds for Artimis to say something. When

he just sat there, smiling, she finally asked him, "Well, find anything interesting?"

"Oh, yeah," he replied.

Val grew impatient as she knew damn well he was intentionally holding something back. "Well, what did you see?" she asked.

Artimis smugly responded, "After we eat, we'll go over to that painting, so you can see for yourself." He gestured to the painting. Artimis with a sly smirk said, "Guess we're in the right location." Val was about to get up to go look at the painting herself when the waitress brought their food. Artimis picked up a fork and started eating when he said to Val, "Don't worry, it will keep until after lunch. That painting has been hanging around this joint for a long time. It isn't going anywhere. Besides, I think we're being watched again." Val sighed and started to eat her meal.

Having finished lunch, Artimis showed Val the painting with the two plaques next to it. Val examined the painting and read the plaques. "Okay, smart guy, but what does it all mean?"

Artimis looked at Val as if she wasn't quite all there, "You're kidding right?" he asked.

Val, with a blank expression on her face, said, "No, I have no idea why you're so excited about this painting?"

Artimis said, "The clue on the Queen of Clubs card is from the Sands Casino. This painting is in the café of the Sands Casino. The clue was, 'The Lady swinging on the Moon will guide your way. Peter is his name I say. A Rat just the same. A present he has for you but only if you can find your way.' Val don't you see? Peter is Peter

Lawford - he's a member of the Rat Pack. I'll bet anything he's got something for you that your mom left with him." Val's face lit up as she realized that Artimis was on to something.

"So now what?" she asked sheepishly. She felt dim-witted about missing the meaning of the clue.

Artimis looked at Val, then snapped his fingers as an idea came to him, "Let's check with the front desk clerk. We can let our two admirers look at this picture for themselves." Val, not sure what Artimis had in mind, decided to follow him, and said, "Okay."

As Val and Artimis approached the front desk, he told her, "Follow my lead." Artimis asked the clerk standing behind the counter, "Sir, may I speak to the manager, please?" Looking up from behind the counter, the man answered, "May I help you?"

Artimis politely said, "Yes, yes, indeed. I'd like to speak to the manager of this casino, please."

The clerk was a young man in his mid-thirties. He was wearing a white, short-sleeved shirt and a solid, bright red tie with "Sands" written across it on a slant. His hair was jet black, cut short, and slicked back. He smiled at Artimis and Val and said, "Yes, of course, one moment sir."

The clerk left the counter and within a minute, he returned and introduced the manager, Al Kline, to Val and Artimis. Al Kline was a hefty, brutish-looking man of German descent, in his mid-fifties. Mr. Kline was a no-nonsense person who did not like the interruption from his daily routine. Mr. Kline forced a smile and asked, "Is there a problem?"

Artimis sized Kline up and knew instantly he was not a person to mince words, "No, no problem, Mr. Kline. We just need to speak with Peter Lawford as soon as we can."

Al Kline smiled, laughed a little, and asked, "Really, and what's your business with Mr. Lawford?"

Artimis spoke in a business- like manner and politely answered, "That's none of your concern for now. Just tell us how we can arrange to meet with Mr. Lawford."

Al Kline hard-heartedly said, "Are you out of your fucking mind? Who the hell do you think you are? You can't just come in here and demand to see Peter Lawford. What are you nuts or something?"

In a raised voice, he told Val and Artimis, "Now get the hell out of here before I throw you two out. If you don't leave these premises now, security will help you find your way out." The manager had his hand on a button underneath the counter, ready to push it to alert security. He smiled at Artimis and Val, showing his perfect white teeth as he finished his short tirade.

Val not intimidated by anyone, especially after shooting the driver of the Lincoln in the forehead, said to the manager in a cold, calm, voice, "Do you know who the fuck I am?"

Kline callously looked at Val and said in a snotty voice, "No, and I really don't care."

Artimis picked up on what Val was attempting to do and butted into the conversation, "Now dear, let's just get Uncle Mickey at the Flamingo to straighten this situation out. I'm certain once this nice gentleman understands who your Uncle Mickey is, well, he'll be more cooperative." Artimis flashed a wide smile at the manager.

Val realized she was almost out of control, she regained her composure, and said to Artimis in a softer, gentler manner, "But, I really don't want to bother Uncle Mickey anymore than I already have, especially with his temper. You know how angry he can get. Remember what he did to the last person who gave us a hard time?" Val's face was somber as she looked at the manager.

Al Kline was not amused but played along mostly out of curiosity and asked, "Okay lady, who are you and who exactly is your Uncle Mickey?"

Before Val had an opportunity to say anything, Artimis answered, "Al, her Uncle Mickey is Mickey Cohen, the Executive Vice President and Director of Archives at the Flamingo. Ever hear of him? And this young lady is the daughter of Benjamin Siegel."

Al Kline responded, "Benjamin Siegel has been dead for more than twenty years now, so what? Everyone knows his two daughters live back East. And besides, she's too young to be his daughter."

Artimis, with a deadpan look, retorted back in an authoritative voice, "So ya think you know everything, huh Mac? This little lady right here is the daughter of Bugsy Siegel. Mickey Cohen was Bugsy's right-hand man. Now, he works with Kerkorian. So unless you lose your holier than thou attitude real quick, you may find yourself filling one of those holes in the desert that Vegas is so famous for. Do you catch my drift?"

The smile on the manager's face remained, "Hey pal you think you're in any position to threaten me? You think you and your barely legal-blond girlfriend can intimidate me?"

Artimis said to Al, "Maybe you're right. Maybe we shouldn't be making threats. But maybe you should give Uncle Mickey a jingle over at the Flamingo, while we wait."

Al Kline frostily said, "Sure thing. Wait here and I'll give him a call." Artimis was suspicious of Kline's suddenly cooperative manner and said, "Hey Al, if you're thinking of calling security, don't bother. We'll leave, but it will get very ugly for you."

Picking up the telephone, Al Kline did not heed Artimis' warning and called security. In less than a minute, two armed security guards were heading toward Val and Artimis. Artimis saw the security guards and yelled to Val, "Run!"

Before the two guards could grab Val and Artimis, they were out the front door in a flash.

Al Kline was right behind Val and Artimis and called out, "Next time you come into this establishment we'll be glad to show you our backroom, and maybe you'll be filling a hole in the desert!" Laughing, Al turned to go back inside and get out of the desert heat.

Not certain what their next step was, Val and Artimis called a cab to pick them up and take them back to the Flamingo. While in the cab, Val asked Artimis, "So how do we get an audience with Peter Lawford now?"

Artimis asked Val, "Do you think Mickey will help us?"

Val responded in a whisper, "Probably not. He wants us to figure this out for ourselves. But I know someone who has a vested interest in our success."

Artimis perked up and asked, "Who's that?"

Val, now talking in a regular voice said, "Jordan Hamilton. I'm calling him as soon as we get back to the room."

Artimis just shrugged his shoulders and said, "Sure, why the hell not?"

Back in their room, Val called Jordan Hamilton. "Mr. Hamilton, Val Benjamin. I need your assistance."

Hamilton, who was sitting at his desk in his Caesars Palace suite, was a bit surprised at hearing Val's voice. "Seriously, Ms. Benjamin, why do you think I'd assist you?"

Val, speaking in a clear relaxed voice, said, "Because we solved one of the riddles that may lead to the deed you're looking to get back."

Hamilton, in a matter of fact tone, replied, "What is it you need?"

Val impersonally said, "We need an introduction to Peter Lawford at the Sands. The manager, Al Kline, is being a dick and had security throw us out this afternoon. He also threatened us with visiting his backroom and filling a hole in the desert next time we step foot in his casino."

Hamilton snarled, "I'm surprised you didn't shoot him in the head!"

Val was not amused at Hamilton's jab and shot back, "*He wasn't trying to kill me.*"

Hamilton ignored Val's comment and continued, "Two of my men, Alfonso and Luigi will pick you up from the Flamingo and escort you to the Sands. In the meantime, I'll make some phone calls. You won't have any more problems with Mr. Kline or his staff, under one condition. Alfonso and Luigi are to be with you at all times."

Val consented and said, "Okay, but make sure that they understand I'm working with you this time and I don't want another threat on my life."

Hamilton responded, "They'll understand. And Ms. Benjamin, please don't kill any more of my men. I received your present and spoke to Jerry. He said you had Bugsy's short temper and that you seem to enjoy killing people. According to Jerry, the apple doesn't fall far from the family tree."

Chapter 14

As Val, Artimis, Alfonso and Luigi approached the front desk at the Sands, Al Kline was waiting for them. Alfonso was a rugged, stocky, broad-shouldered man, with thick dark hair and captivating brown eyes, who exuded confidence. Luigi was slightly taller than Alfonso and was slender. His eyes were so dark they appeared black as coal. He wore a light grey suit, white shirt and red tie. Luigi looked more like a GQ model than a professional bodyguard and hit man.

Luigi immigrated to America when he was sixteen. He wanted a part of the American dream; to be a successful, wealthy businessman. He became a part of the Giancana Family at age eighteen. Despite numerous suggestions to anglicize his first name from Luigi to Lewis, he refused to do so.

Alfonso was born and raised in Chicago, Illinois. As a child, his father was one of the union bosses that controlled Chicago labor. Alfonso was introduced to organized crime at a chance political meeting between Sam Giancana and Richard Daley during John Kennedy's presidential campaign. Alfonso worked for Jordan Hamilton's syndicate. He worked his way up the ranks because of his affiliation with Giancana and his father's connection with the unions.

Nervously and with a quiver in his voice, Al Kline said, "Mr. Lawford is doing a photo shoot out front by the marquee with the other fellows. I'll have Mr. Ebbins, his manager; escort you so there won't be any trouble for you."

Milton "Milt" Ebbins was Peter Lawford's personal manager. Ebbins' partnership with Lawford brought him into close association with the Kennedy clan.

In 1961, Lawford and Ebbins formed *Chrislaw Productions* - which was named after Peter's son Christopher and produced the 1963 action film, *Johnny Cool,* staring Henry Silva and Elizabeth Montgomery. Lawford also produced the 1965 Patty Duke film, *Billie,* as well as two films with Sammy Davis, Jr., *Salt and Pepper* and *One More Time.* Milt, in his mid-fifties, was slightly heavyset weighing about 225 pounds, with a jolly face. He was balding in the middle of his hair line, wore large black rimmed glasses and stood about 5'8" tall. He was wearing a grey blazer, black dress slacks, a white shirt that hung slightly over his belt, and a narrow, solid navy blue tie.

Artimis stared at Kline with cold hatred. Val kept her eyes trained on the front desk clerk. Artimis took only one step before he rammed his fist into Kline's mouth, splitting his lips and sending a spurt of crimson blood down the front of his white shirt.

"You bastard," yelled Kline.

"That's for threatening me with a visit to your backroom," said Artimis. Another intense, violent movement and Artimis' next blow was to his mid section with his leg, sending Kline to his knees, gasping and choking for air. "And that's for having security try to throw us out of here the last time we visited you." Artimis, with his elbow, gave one more final blow to Kline's head knocking him down - he was out cold.

Val, surprised by Artimis' sudden rage, smiled from ear to ear and said, "Thank you. Your cooperation is most appreciated." She glanced at Alfonso and Luigi and then at the desk clerk and Mr. Ebbins. "Anyone else has something they want to say?" she asked.

Mr. Ebbins and the front desk clerk shook their heads no. "Remind me never to make you mad," Val said to Artimis.

Mr. Ebbins gestured to the four to follow him and said, "Right this way." Ebbins escorted what looked like a tourist group through the casino and outside to the front of the complex. Passing three security guards, Ebbins merely flashed his infectious smile as they approached the marquee. Standing in front of the marquee were two photographers, Dean Martin, Frank Sinatra, Peter Lawford, Sammy Davis, Jr. and Joey Bishop. Also with the group were several make-up artists who were making certain the five looked fresh in the heat of the day.

The Rat Pack was a group of actors originally centered on Humphrey Bogart. Virginia, a friend of Bogart, was a member of the pack at the beginning. But after Bogart's death in 1957, they called themselves "the summit" or "the clan," featuring Frank Sinatra, Dean Martin, Sammy Davis, Jr., Peter Lawford, and Joey Bishop. They appeared together on stage and in films in the early 60s, including the movie *Ocean's 11*. It was Milt Ebbins who was credited for Lawford being cast in *Ocean's 11* as well as *The Longest Day*. "The Rat Pack" was a term used by journalists and outsiders, although the name stuck and remained with them. Sinatra, Martin, and Davis were regarded as the group's lead members. By this time, Virginia was on the outs with the remaining members and was not welcomed.

Many times, when one of the members was scheduled to give a performance, the rest of the Pack would show up for an impromptu show, causing much excitement among audiences, which resulted in return visits. Sinatra, Martin, Lawford, and Davis sold out almost all of their appearances, and people came to Vegas in droves just to be part of the Rat Pack entertainment experience. People would sleep in their car or hotel lobbies if they could not get a room. "The Rat Pack" turned Vegas into a party town.

Their appearances were of unparalleled value because the city always became flooded with high rollers, like whales who were wealthy gamblers that routinely left a part of their fortunes in the casinos' coffers.

Peter Lawford was a brother in law of President John F. Kennedy. Sinatra affectionately referred to Lawford as the "Brother-in-Lawford." "The Rat Pack" campaigned for Kennedy and the Democrats. They even appeared at the Democratic National Convention in Los Angeles on July 11, 1960. Milt Ebbins was a well-connected show business manager who was a liaison between Hollywood and the Kennedy White House. He was a favorite of President John F. Kennedy and a frequent guest at the White House and on Air Force One.

According to close friends of Lawford, in March, 1962, he asked Sinatra if Kennedy could be a guest at Sinatra's Palm Springs house. Sinatra went to great expense, including construction of a helipad, to accommodate the President. Robert F. Kennedy, however, advised his brother to sever his ties with Sinatra because of the entertainer's association with Mafia figures such as Sam Giancana.

Heeding Bobby's advice, the President cancelled his plans to stay at Sinatra's residence. John Kennedy chose to stay at Bing

Crosby's estate instead. Since Crosby was a rival of Sinatra, this infuriated the hot tempered crooner. He blamed Lawford for President Kennedy's insult and never said a good word about Lawford again.

Virginia saw the feud between Sinatra and Lawford as an opportunity and seized the moment. During one of the President's trips to Vegas, Virginia persuaded Lawford's manager, Milt Ebbins, to arrange for her to meet President Kennedy. Ebbins came through and arranged for Virginia to be seated with President Kennedy and Marilyn Monroe at a table for their show at the Copacabana Club. After everyone had a few drinks, a photographer took their picture together. Virginia, always scheming, had prearranged for the photographer to take the incriminating photo.

Mr. Ebbins took Val, Artimis, Alfonso and Luigi to where Peter Lawford was doing a photo shoot with Sammy Davis, Jr., Dean Martin, Joey Bishop, and Frank Sinatra. The five of them were standing in front of the Sands' marquee. The marquee had all five names listed. Once the photo shoot was concluded, Ebbins spoke to Peter and said, "Peter, this young lady would like a word with you."

"What's this about, Milt?" Peter asked.

Milt said solemnly, "I'm not sure sir, but Al gave me clear instructions that she was to meet you."

Peter Lawford was the first actor to kiss Elizabeth Taylor on camera, and the last to speak to Marilyn Monroe before she died. He organized the infamous 45th birthday party in 1962 for Kennedy at Madison Square Garden where Monroe sang "Happy Birthday" to the President. It was Ebbins who gave her a push onstage at Madison

Square Garden as she went out to sing her sultry version of the song.

Suave and charming, the debonair Lawford enjoyed a reputation as a jet-setting playboy who was a heavy drinker. In 1954, he married Patricia Kennedy, sister of then-Senator John F. Kennedy. The two divorced in 1966 after Peter admitted to having several affairs.

Val was aware of Peter's reputation as a womanizer from working at MGM. He was dressed in a dark navy blue suit, wearing a white shirt and a narrow black tie. He looked at Val suspiciously and said, "What can I do for you, sweetie?"

Val said, "Thank you for taking the time to meet with me, Mr. Lawford. I believe you have a something for me."

Artimis' attention was focused on Frank Sinatra, Dean Martin and Sammy Davis, Jr. who were gawking at her with a look of "who the hell is this chick?"

Lawford, already in a foul mood from standing in heat for the photo shoot, agitatedly retorted, "What the hell are you talking about, lady? I don't know you. What do you want?"

Hearing the commotion, Martin in a cold, callused voice shouted over, "Is there a problem, Pete?" Lawford not knowing what to expect, but knowing Milt had escorted the group, called back, "No, no problem. Go ahead. I'll catch up with you guys." Martin did not give it a second thought, turned, and walked away with the other members of the Rat Pack.

Artimis, who was used to being around Hollywood actors and actresses, ignored the group as they strolled past him. Val answered, "My name is Valentina. I believe you knew my mother, Virginia Hill."

The comment got Lawford's attention, "Really, what makes you so certain I knew Virginia?"

Val was in no position to play games. She simply stated, "Look, I know you knew Virginia because I have photos of you with her." Val, of course, was bluffing.

Lawford not knowing if Val actually had photos with him and Virginia, said, "Let me see your left shoulder."

Val responded, "Why?"

"Because I need to make certain you're who you say you are. You are not the first young woman to approach me claiming to be the daughter of Virginia Hill. The others couldn't prove it. So, young lady, I've become very cautious, and unless you want to show me your left shoulder, we have nothing further to discuss."

Val lowered her shirt exposing her left shoulder. The tattoo of the Florentine "F," surrounded by the suits in a diamond shape, was there for Peter to see.

Peter, with a deep breath, said to Val, "So, you're the one." Milt was listening as Lawford continued, "Here's how this is gonna go down. You'll be my guest tonight for our 11:00 p.m. show. Tickets will be waiting for you and your friends here at the will call window. Afterwards, I'll give you what you what I've been holding for you. Milt you got all that? We're done here."

Peter called out to Sammy who was still hanging around talking with the photographer's crew and said, "Wait up." He turned and walked away without saying another word.

Seeing that Lawford left Val to join the other members of The

Rat Pack, Artimis, Luigi and Alfonso walked over towards Mr. Ebbins and Val without any discussion.

Ebbins asked curtly, "Did your meeting go well with Mr. Lawford?" Val eyed Luigi and said curtly, "Yes."

Luigi looked at Ebbins and stated, "This is none of your business, pal."

Ebbins was smug and responded to Luigi's rudeness, "Oh contraire, it is my business when Al Kline is as unsettled as he was by the phone call he received from your 'Uncle Mickey." He continued, "Lady, I sure hope you know what you're doing because you've upset a lot of powerful people around here."

Val, simply said, "Good, I want them to be. Maybe Mr. Kline will remember to be a little more respectful the next time we meet."

Ebbins said, "Oh, I'm sure he'll remember," and motioned the group to move on.

The group finally reached the front door to the Sands Casino where Val and her cohorts parted ways with Mr. Ebbins.

Chapter 15

Jordan Hamilton's suite at Caesars Palace was magnificent. The suite was thirty-five hundred square feet, larger than most homes. It was furnished lavishly with oriental rugs, leather sofas and three separate master suites complete with Roman tubs and double sink vanities. Each bedroom had its own bath. The view from Jordan's suite was The Flamingo directly across the street. To Jordan, The Flamingo was an eyesore. He would have preferred a view of the desert to that of the pink monstrosity.

Mickey Cohen entered Jordan's suite with an agenda to settle a score from two decades ago. Years later, Cohen remembered: "Siegel would throw me ten grand, twenty-five grand... the biggest was forty grand. There were no books kept or explanations. All he would say is, 'Here, this is for you'." Jordan Hamilton was present one night when Siegel threw Mickey twenty grand. Hamilton saw the cash sitting on his coffee table when he arrived at Mickey's home for a business meeting.

Shortly after the meeting Mickey noticed the cash was missing from the table. He confronted Hamilton who denied taking the cash. The two rarely spoke after that evening.

Cohen had enemies in the mob and survived many attempts on his life, including several he thought were ordered by Hamilton.

Mickey was greeted by two of Jordan's men, padded down and was told that Mr. Hamilton would be right with him. Jordan entered the area where Mickey was waiting and said, "Mickey, please sit down," gesturing toward the suite's living room couch.

Mickey sat on the couch and Jordan sat in an adjacent love seat. Mickey started the conversation, "Jordan you really created a mess, sending Tony Ianotti to kill Val." He continued, "I got the FBI to back off for now. I promised them I would hand over Sam Shaw's killer. What the hell were you thinking killing Shaw?"

Hamilton looked Mickey straight in the eye and said defiantly, "Tony is dead. That pinky finger sent to me was his. Your trigger happy lady friend buried him in the desert. Tell the FBI they can find his body near the burnt Lincoln. And by the way, Shaw's death was a direct order from Joe."

Mickey looked perplexed by Hamilton's reference to Joe. "Why? What did Shaw have to do with any of this?"

Hamilton leaned closer to Mickey as he spoke to him. "You know Bobby is running for president this year. Joe is worried that Virginia had incriminating evidence that could ruin Bobby's candidacy. Virginia already blackmailed Bobby back in sixty-five."

Mickey listened intently then interrupted Hamilton and said, "Yeah, but she's dead. What is Joe so uptight about?"

Hamilton continued, "My understanding is Virginia had the deeds to the El Rancho Casino with his signature transferring ownership to Jake Katleman and other proof that Joe ordered the place to be torched."

Mickey asked Hamilton, "How did Virginia get the deed to begin with?"

Hamilton said, "Joe acquired an ownership interest in the El Rancho from Los Angeles businessman Walter Guzzardi in 1946. Joe, as a favor for the Teamsters Union and Meyer Lansky, transferred his ownership interest in the El Rancho to Katleman in 1947. Joe's interest in the El Rancho from Guzzardi was never recorded. Neither was the transfer of his ownership to Katleman. Virginia approached Katleman after Joe gave the deed to him and persuaded Katleman to give the deed to her in return for an interest in The Flamingo. Virginia contacted Joe and tried to sell the deed back to him in 1965. Joe didn't want to pay her as it was worthless at that time. He had destroyed the deed transferring part ownership from Guzzardi to him back in 1950. Virginia told Joe that someday he would regret his decision, and she would make the documents public record. Joe wasn't too concerned about it until Bobby started his presidential campaign."

The El Rancho Casino was the first hotel and casino complex to open on the highway from L.A. that led into downtown Las Vegas. Built in 1941, it was the first major casino and hotel built on the Strip.

"That's it? That's what all of this is about?" Mickey inquired.

Hamilton, still leaning in close to Mickey, said, "No, that's not all of it. Meyer wants his money back. He suspected Virginia had hid it all along."

Mickey still looked a little puzzled. Mickey waited patiently for Hamilton to continue.

Hamilton leaned back in the love seat and smiled, "Meyer is backing Bobby's campaign, Mickey. Campaigns cost money. Meyer wants his stolen money back to help fund Bobby's campaign. Joe and Meyer made deals with the Teamsters Union leaders to sweeten the pot for certain political favors."

"So, you blew up Shaw because he was a potential witness?" Mickey asked.

"Shaw was the only person other than Thornton who had possession of the envelope. Joe was concerned Shaw may have looked into the envelope to see what was in it. Joe doesn't want any loose ends. I convinced him that, for now, we let Val figure out the clues and then move-in."

Mickey was becoming persuaded by Hamilton's story. He asked, "Why hasn't anyone gone after Thornton? He had access to the envelope, too."

Hamilton said, "Because Thornton is a wealthy attorney who is actually backing Bobby. Joe trusts him. Hell, Joe even likes him."

Mickey said, "So you made a deal with Val not to harm her so long as she gives you the deed and the other documents concerning the El Rancho. But she doesn't know Joe wants the two million dollars. Nice. What happens if Val and her friend find the two million? " Mickey was not aware that Val had removed thirty thousand from the envelope.

"Joe said he would take care of it. I'm smart enough not to ask any questions when it comes to Joe. Besides, my deal is with Val. I didn't say anything to her about Joe and neither should you. Why are you helping her anyways?"

"Let's just say Joe and I have a similar interest in the money Virginia stole from Meyer. Two million is a lot of dough - - not a mere 20 grand," Mickey added for good measure. Hamilton smiled, knowing full well what the reference to the twenty grand meant.

"Do we have a deal then? I leave Val alone until she finds the deed and other documents and gives them to me. You let her keep looking for the money. If she finds it, you and Joe work it out."

Mickey was still confused about Iannotti screwing up the hit at the MGM parking lot. "Jordan, who was the trigger person at the MGM studio? Certainly it wasn't Tony?" he asked.

Hamilton leaned toward Mickey again and, in a slow, low voice that was almost a whisper, he said, "The Mechanic." Hamilton, after answering Mickey's question, backed off and smiled. "Doesn't it bother you that The Mechanic missed Val?" Mickey asked Hamilton.

Mickey continued, "The Mechanic never misses and never leaves lose ends."

Hamilton pulled out a Don Pepin cigar from his suit jacket's pocket, cut the end off with a cigar cutter, but did not light it. He put the cigar in his mouth, only to take it out, and said to Mickey, "No, not at all. It was only a matter of time when he would miss his mark. Besides, he wasn't supposed to kill the girl. He was only supposed to get the envelope. You know he sometimes will shoot his gun for the fun of it."

Mickey stood up from the couch at the same time Hamilton rose from the love seat. Mickey smiled and extended his right hand to shake Hamilton's hand saying, "Sounds reasonable to me, we have a deal."

As Mickey left Jordan's suite, he thought to himself "That was way too easy. Something else is up." Mickey knew the Mechanic would never miss an easy target, especially when Val was unaware that he was shooting at her. No, Mickey was certain someone else had a hand in this mess. Someone, he thought, who knew about the hit and wanted to protect Valentina.

Mickey arrived at his office at The Flamingo. He immediately called Peter Atwood. Agent Atwood listened as Mickey told him about the location of Tony Iannotti's body and that Iannotti was responsible for Shaw's death.

Agent Atwood was not satisfied with Mickey's explanation for Shaw's demise. "Mickey, why was Shaw the target of a mafia hit?" he asked.

Mickey was disappointed that Atwood was pressing the issue. "Look, Atwood, the envelope that Shaw delivered to Val was thought to contain sensitive information about certain individuals who shall remain anonymous for now. Unfortunately for Shaw, it did not even have that information. Valentina and Artimis are using the contents of the envelope to track it down, however, and possibly also two million dollars in stolen cash. So you gotta back off the case and leave it be for now. Just report it as a mistaken identity for the hit."

Agent Atwood decided to play along with Mickey for the second time. "I'll do as you ask for now on the condition that you continue to keep me posted about Ms. Benjamin and Mr. Sylver. I want to know their whereabouts at all times. This case may appear to be closed, but it's not over."

Atwood was suspicious of Mickey's explanation but did not want to push the issue of why he thought the hit was botched. He decided to give Mickey some more leeway in the hopes of arresting several of the mobs' head honchos.

Chapter 16

The music from the band came in ever rising waves as it neared its crescendo. The band had never played better, never had more passion. The performers' faces glistened with sweat as they poured their souls into each note. The audience sat captivated by the performance, knowing they were experiencing the magic of a legendary group.

The show at the Copa Room was an outstanding extravaganza of show girls known as "The Copa Girls" and, of course, The Rat Pack. The Copa Room, named for the famed Copacabana in New York City, was the entertainment nightclub showroom at the Sands in Las Vegas. The musical director was the legendary Antonio Morelli. It was noteworthy for the large number of popular entertainers who performed there: Count Basie, Ella Fitzgerald, Judy Garland, Lena Horne, Jimmy Durante, Tony Bennett, Nat King Cole, Peggy Lee, and Bobby Darin, among others. The Copa Room was also the recording venue for several live albums, including Frank Sinatra's *Sinatra at the Sands*, Sammy Davis, Jr.'s *That's All!* and *The Sounds of '66*, and Dean Martin's *Live at the Sands Hotel - An Evening of Music, Laughter and Hard Liquor.*

After experiencing the show of a lifetime, Val, Artimis, Luigi, and Alfonso waited until all the other patrons had left. They were still sitting at their table when they were approached by Mr. Ebbins. Usually a jolly man, he looked at the four with disdain, wondering still what stronghold they had over Al Kline and Peter Lawford to warrant such special treatment. Kline would never have let anyone smack him around the way Sylver did; not without retaliation. Yet Kline gave the order that no one was to harm Artimis and Val, or even remotely upset them.

Ebbins said to the group, "Come with me. I'll escort you to Mr. Lawford's dressing room."

Peter Lawford, held a glass of bourbon in one hand and a cigarette in the other, and stood in a dark corner of his otherwise well - lit dressing room. Staring out through the smoke and semi-darkness he looked at Val and Artimis, who sat waiting for him to say something.

But he said nothing at first. There was only silence.

Finally, after a few moments, he said, "Thank you, Milt, that will be all for now." With that, Milt Ebbins politely turned and exited the dressing room.

Now in his private sanctuary, he seemed very distant. Val and Artimis, judging from the ambiance in Lawford's dressing room, thought, as did Alfonso and Luigi, who stood nearby, that it was a bad idea to try and force a conversation with Lawford when he was in a sullen silence. A mood that most people didn't realize had hardly been uncommon during the last month.

Lawford's dressing room was more like a suite with a wet bar stocked with whiskey and bourbon than a dressing room. On one end near the entrance was a couch and love seat. Between the couch and love seat was a glass coffee table with a wood frame. Towards the back of the suite, on a wall, were bright, ball-shaped lighted mirrors and across the other side a full closet with several suits, dress shirts, ties, and shoes. In front of the makeup table were several photos of famous people Lawford socialized with. There was even a photo of Lawford with President Kennedy from when they played golf together at the Desert Inn's Golf Course. Most of the photos were in black and white, a handful were in color.

"Virginia wanted me to give this to you," Lawford said as he handed Val a large brown envelope with the same symbol on the outside as the envelope from the attorney.

"What's in it?" Val asked as she took the envelope from Lawford.

Lawford eyed Val who wore a red formal gown. Her hair and makeup were flawless, and she radiated a sexy, sophisticated look. Artimis, Luigi, and Alfonso wore black tuxedos, and each looked handsome in his own way. "Look lady, I don't know, and I don't want to know. Just before Virginia died she asked me to hold on to this and to give it to her kid when the time was right. I had no idea what she was talking about. Hell, I didn't even know she had a kid. She made me swear not to open the package or talk about it to anyone. I knew she was serious because of her reputation. It's a known fact that people who crossed her died. So, here it is. Have a nice life, kid. Oh, one more thing - Virginia asked me to give you a message. She said to 'say hello to Bobby for her'."

Val was holding the envelope in her left hand as she looked Lawford in the eye and asked, "Bobby who?"

Peter was shaking his head back and forth and grinning with a *you've got to be kidding* look as he walked out of the dressing room, and waved good bye. As he strolled out the door he said, "See ya, kiddo," and kept on walking. Had it been any other woman, Lawford probably would have made a play to get inside her pants. But Lawford was smart enough to stay away from Valentina.

Val, undaunted, walked briskly after him, "Hey, wait a minute. I've got more questions for you," Val yelled at him just after he exited the doorway. Lawford, with a glance over his shoulder, stopped mid-stride. He had heard that tone in a female's voice before. Some call it a sixth sense - the mind's ability to know when something isn't quite right. Lawford turned around with a look of fear in his eyes and said to Val, "Come with me and we'll talk, in private, alone."

Val, without hesitating handed the envelope to Artimis. "Meet me in the lounge. Don't you dare think of opening it," Val said as her eyes grew wide.   Looking straight at Alfonso and Luigi, she said, "That goes for you two, too. If you do, I'll kill all three of you and don't think I won't!"

Artimis took the envelope from Val, glared at her, and then looked at Luigi and Alfonso. He said, "Come on, you heard the lady. Let's go up front and have a cocktail in the lounge." Artimis was not happy with the rage displayed by Val.

Val and Lawford sat at a private table just out of earshot from everyone else. "No amount of lye could cleanse the stench of Virginia Hill and the swath of ugliness she brought onto those whose lives she touched," Lawford started. "She was an evil, wicked woman who manipulated people like pawns on a chess board." Now young lady, what do you want to know?"

Val looked at Lawford with tearful eyes, overwhelmed by what she had just heard and the tone in which it was said. "What exactly did Virginia Hill do to you to warrant your malice?"

As soon as the waiter brought their drinks and departed, Lawford looked deep into Val's piercing blue eyes and said, "Virginia was a party animal who loved to drink and screw. She had connections with Sinatra's people. Frank allowed her to hang around whenever she wanted. No one questioned Frank or his motives. One night Virginia approached me in my dressing room. I was alone at the time. Her breath reeked of booze, and she was plastered, totally wasted. She told me she couldn't trust anyone but me and wanted me to do her a favor. I didn't want anything to do with her so I said, 'No.' She didn't like being told no, and she pulled out the envelope I handed to you earlier. With a cat like quickness, she thrust the envelope in my gut and told me to keep it safe. Virginia wasn't someone you messed around with. She told me that if I ever opened the envelope I would be dead - that she had paid people to watch me to make certain that seal was never broken except by you. She paced around, screaming that if I didn't help her, I would end up like Jack and Ben."

Val interrupted Lawford, so he took a deep breath and a sip from his glass of bourbon, and asked, "Jack who?"

Lawford put his glass down and laughed. "Are you really that naïve? Jack Kennedy of course," he said. She would make gestures with her hand as if pointing a gun at my head and pulling the trigger. Bang, she would say in a loud voice. 'Fuck with me and I'll have your head blown apart like they did to Jack and Ben'."

Lawford shook his head back and forth before continuing.

"No way was I going to take any chances. So I agreed to her demands - even after she died. I've had that package for years, hidden in my safe. Never once took it out until today."

Lawford picked up his glass of bourbon and quickly gulped it down. He stood up, looked at Val, and said, "We're finished. I have nothing else to say to you," and he abruptly left the table.

Artimis started to move toward Val when he saw Lawford leave the table. Before he could take another step, she motioned for him to wait, secretly pointing at Alfonso and Luigi.

Val got up from the table and took a seat next to Artimis at the table in the lounge where the three of them were sitting, "Okay, boys, time to see if what your boss wants is in this package."

Val took the envelope, which was sitting on Artimis's lap covered by his hand. Slowly and carefully, she opened the parcel and deposited the contents on the table. The contents contained a piece of paper with a handwritten note, some stock certificates for IBM, AT&T, Coca-Cola, General Electric, two more black and white photos of Virginia and Ben together, and a key. The certificate for IBM indicated there were five hundred shares, AT&T was for one thousand shares, Coca-Cola was for one thousand shares, and General Electric was for two thousand shares. That was the entire contents of the envelope. The stock certificates were all titled in Val's name under the Gift to Minors Act. The key was flat, similar to a safe deposit box key, but not exactly the same. It was slightly thicker and had a decorative top like those of a skeleton key. It was unique just the same. The photos appeared odd. Val could not quite determine what was wrong with them other than they seemed off. Something about their tone didn't seem right.

Luigi and Alfonso picked up each item and vigilantly examined them. Val and Artimis did not bother them as they took turns looking at each document and looked into the opened envelope to see if there was anything else tucked inside.

Val was not too pleased with Alfonso as he put his high ball glass on one of the photos from the second envelope she just received. Apparently Luigi and Alfonso made it clear they were going to see everything in Val's possession.

"Hey asshole," Val yelled at Alfonso, "Take that fuckin' glass off that photo. What kinda pig are you?"

Alfonso was in no mood to get into a pissing contest with Val and he quietly removed the glass from the photo. Val picked up the photo and wiped the water ring from it. The damage was already done. The water ring left a mark. Val put everything back into the first envelope quickly.

Luigi grabbed the envelope from Val's hand and said, "I'll hang on to that until we see the boss."

Val warily watched each of the two men. Luigi put all of the documents back into the envelope but left the key on the table. He called out to the bartender, "Hey bud, you got a telephone back there I can use?" At three o'clock in the morning, the bartender didn't move too quickly. He picked up a telephone from behind the bar and simply put it in front of Luigi.

Luigi's using his finger to turn the rotary dial, dialed the number. A voice on the other end responded, "What do you got?"

Luigi, in a gruff voice, replied, "Not much and nothing that seems of use to you, except a key."

The voice on the other end of the phone line said, "Bring the two over with the stuff."

"Yes sir," was all that Luigi said as he hung up the phone. Luigi stood up from the table and said, "Come on everybody, time to go see the boss." As if on cue, Alfonso, Val, and Artimis got up from the table and headed towards the door. Artimis took a C note from his front right side pocket and left it on the table to pay for the drinks and a nice tip for the bartender.

Alfonso reached forward to take the key, but Val grabbed it before he could. "Not so fast pal, this is my stuff," Val snapped at Alfonso. Alfonso let Val keep the key. Luigi still kept a tight grasp of the envelope.

The rising crescent moon made the stones of the marble statutes at Caesars Palace gleam eerily, while the haze surrounding them exuded an air of menace. Jordan sat impatiently, waiting for Luigi and Alfonso to bring Val and Artimis to his suite. The twenty minutes it took for the group to arrive seemed like an eternity. Finally, Luigi knocked on the door as another bodyguard let him and the others into the suite.

Without hesitation, Hamilton quickly rifled through the envelope and looked at the documents given to him by Luigi. "This is it?" he exclaimed with disappointment.

Luigi who had handed Jordan the packages for him to examine

said, "Nothing else sir, except a key in Ms. Benjamin's possession." Val opened her hand to show Hamilton the key. Hamilton eyed the key in Val's hand but did not attempt to take it.

After a few minutes, Jordan looked at the handwritten note. "Damn bitch," is all he said. His eyes widened revealing that they were bloodshot.

Val, seeing desperation in Hamilton's face, spoke up, saying, "Mr. Hamilton, if I may have my papers perhaps Artimis and I can keep searching to find what you want."

Hamilton did not say a word. He just gestured to Luigi to give Val the envelope and for her and Artimis to leave. Hamilton, in an irritated voice, said to his men, "Luigi, Alfonso let the two of them go. They can walk back to their place."

Artimis and Val left Jordan Hamilton's suite and were in the elevator heading down to the ground level when Artimis, who had loosened his bow tie and undid the top button of his tux shirt, asked Val, "So what's written on the note?" Val handed the note to Artimis who started reading it out loud: "By now, you have probably been told what a bitch I can be. The Queen of Clubs will help you with part of the information you need. If you stop now, you will have a lot of money from the stocks I put in your name. But if you keep looking, your fortune will vastly expand. Beware, though, for what you find will put your life in much more danger."

As Val and Artimis strolled across Las Vegas Boulevard toward the Flamingo, Val looked at Artimis and said, "Time to head back to LA. I need to talk some more with my mom about my adoption and see if she knows more than she's letting on."

Artimis did not argue and agreed with Val, only saying, "Yeah, I should get back to the office and get some work done." He added, "What do you think that stock is worth?"

Val shrugged, "I don't know, but I'll find out soon enough."

Chapter 17

Martha sipped her cup of coffee, as she sat at the kitchen table looking through the latest issue of *Good Housekeeping Magazine*. This was just another day of the same old grind for Martha. As she was engrossed in her thoughts looking through the articles and new recipes, Val entered quietly through the back door.

"Hi mom," Val said, greeting her mother with a cheerful, yet reserved demeanor.

"Oh, hi dear," Martha replied back, without looking up. "How did your search in Vegas turn out?" Martha asked as she peered upwards at Val.

Val was puzzled by the calmness of her mother after the ordeal she and her father had been put through by Hamilton. "Mom, are you all right?" Val inquired.

Martha, with a smile, looked at Val with tender loving eyes and said, "No, not really dear, but the doctor prescribed me some Valium. It seems to be working, so I don't become hysterical."

"Mom I need to talk to you about Virginia Hill and her brother, my uncle, Chick. It's important for me to understand who and what I'm dealing with. Artimis and I are making progress but we've hit a few obstacles."

Martha put her magazine aside, looked directly at Val, and said, "I really don't have a lot of information, dear, but ask away."

Val began by asking, "How did you ever get involved with Bugsy Segal and Virginia Hill in the first place?"

Martha, took another sip of coffee, put the cup down, and said,

"Your father and I first met Chick at the Brown Derby. We were having dinner to celebrate our wedding anniversary. Chick had too much to drink and bumped into our table. My glass of Merlot got knocked over and spilled all over me. Apparently, Chick was a regular at the Brown Derby and was known to be obnoxious when he had too much to drink. The waiter immediately came over to see what all of the commotion was about. The waiter made sure we were okay and reprimanded Chick for his drunkenness."

Martha continued, "A few days later an envelope with a note card and two hundred dollars was left at our front door. It was from Chick. The note was an apology and the two hundred was for my dress and for your dad and me to have another dinner, courtesy of him."

"What happened after that?" Val interrupted.

Martha smiled, and said, "About a week later, your father and I returned to the Brown Derby for dinner. Chick saw us and came over to our table. He again apologized profusely. Your father, not knowing who Chick was or who he was related to, invited him to join us for dinner. To my surprise, he accepted the invitation."

"During dinner, Chick asked about our previous dinner. Your father told Chick it was our wedding anniversary. Chick then asked how long we had been married, if we had any children, and so forth."

"Didn't you think it was odd for a complete stranger to ask such personal questions?" Val interjected.

Martha responded, "Of course we did. What else do you want to know?" Martha asked.

Val pressed the issue further and said, "I still don't understand how you got involved with Virginia and Bugsy."

Martha spoke directly, but her eyes glazed as she remembered the past, "I never met Bugsy, I only met Virginia. You were only four months old when Bugsy was killed."

"Shortly after our dinner conversation with Chick, he invited your father and I to meet Virginia for lunch. We were, of course, excited to be meeting a famous person, so we agreed to meet her. We met at a discrete restaurant to avoid any embarrassment for Virginia. When we met Virginia she was very pregnant, and Chick made us swear that we would not tell anyone about her condition. During lunch, Virginia asked your father and me if we would be interested in adopting you."

Val interrupted again and asked, "Why did Virginia ask you to adopt me?"

Martha, still under the influence of the Valium, said, "Apparently, Chick told Virginia about his encounter with your father and me. It was Chick's suggestion that Virginia consider giving up her child for adoption. During our lunch meeting, Virginia said she had your father and me investigated by a private detective. So, after she met us, it was decided by everyone that we would adopt you. Everything was done very hush, hush - very discrete and secretive. We wanted a child, and I was unable to conceive, so it seemed like a good idea, especially after Bugsy was killed. From the time you were born until a few weeks ago, no one knew you were adopted."

"Why not?" Val asked. "What happened to Chick? What

happened to Virginia?" Martha looked at her empty coffee cup, got up, and went to the refrigerator. She opened the door and took out a bottle of white wine. Removing the cork, she grabbed a goblet from the cabinet, and poured a glass. "Would you like a glass, dear?" Martha asked.

"A little early to be drinking isn't it mom?" Val replied.

"I'll take that as a no," responded Martha, placing the bottle back into the refrigerator.

Sitting back down at the kitchen table, Martha swirled the wine in the glass and looked straight at Val. Without hesitation, Martha declared, "Virginia was a self-centered person. She cared nothing for anyone but herself. You were only four months old when Bugsy was killed. Virginia took off to Paris. She never once tried to contact us. She never once asked to see you or even asked how you were doing. Chick was worse than she was. After the adoption, I read in the paper that he was arrested and ended up in prison. I never thought about him again after that. For all I know, he's either dead or still in prison. I read a few years later that Virginia remarried and gave birth to a son named Peter. I never gave much thought to Virginia after that until I read about her death two years ago."

"Are you sorry you adopted me?" Val asked Martha.

Looking hurt and dismayed by the question, Martha got up, went over to Val and gave her a big hug. "No, of course not, I love you so much. I just wish you weren't going through all this shit."

Val was surprised by her mom's vulgarity as she never had heard her swear before. Remembering that her mother had said something about a guardian she asked, "Mom, you said something about me having a guardian. What did you mean by that?"

Martha sat down in her seat, took a swig of wine, and said, "Virginia was known to be a conniver and a schemer. Someone you could not trust. She always wanted something. She must have had a lot of dirt on someone because whoever it was, they were watching from afar and doing so to provide for you."

Val, not understanding her mother's ramblings, thought the combination of the Valium and the wine must be affecting her cognitive thinking. Val said, "I'm not sure I understand what you're saying, mom."

"Damn it, Val! I don't know who this person was who helped your father and me throughout the years. As I told you, someone was watching and making certain you got whatever you needed or wanted. It was creepy and frightening. Not to mention having a complete stranger appear at my door and hold me at gun point. I'm done answering questions. You need to leave." Val realized that her question about "the guardian" triggered an unintended emotional response from her mom.

She got up from the table, gave her mother a kiss on the cheek, and said, "I love you, mom," and left.

Chapter 18

Val returned to her apartment to find Artimis waiting inside. "How the hell did you get in?"

Artimis flashed a wide grin and said, "Annette let me in so that I could wait for you. She was on her way to work."

Val could smell the distinct odor of pot as she made her way further into the apartment. "You could of at least opened a window to air this place out - - jerk."

Artimis smiled, "You can thank your landlady for me. She handed me a few joints when I was walking to your place."

Val did not say anything as she lit a candle to hide the smell. Artimis' eyes were dilated from the weed and Val was not in the mood to verbally spar with him.

"Val, what is your problem? Seriously, we spend time in Vegas together, got shot at, chased by thugs, threatened by Mafioso characters, I watched you shoot someone in the head at point blank range, I beat up a manager at a casino, and you still don't trust me!"

"You're such an ass," Val replied. "Besides, I've got to get some more answers to this mess."

Not wanting to waste any more time with Artimis, she said, as she moved about her apartment, "Well, for your information, the stock certificates are worth more than five hundred thousand dollars." Thinking to herself out loud she murmured, "Where the hell did I put that attorney's business card?"

Rummaging through a dresser drawer she cried out, "Eureka! Found it." Val examined the card Sam Shaw had handed her just prior to his demise. The card was a simple white business card that read, "Thornton, Mender and Bigelow, Sam Shaw, Esq., Senior Partner." Val noticed the card contained a Chicago address and telephone number.

Still in a coma-like stupor, Artimis turned over and said, "Now what?"

Val shot him a glance of malcontent and responded, "I'm going to Chicago."

"Chicago?" Artimis, suddenly more alert, asked, "Why Chicago?"

"Because the attorney who gave me that envelope was from Chicago," Val retorted. "Someone at that law firm has answers and I'm going to get them."

After a few moments, the amount that Val told Artimis finally sunk in. "Did you say five hundred thousand dollars?" he asked.

Val flashed him a wicked smile and said, "Yes, I did. More than half a million bucks." Artimis just sat on the sofa with a smirk on his face."

Chicago in late May can be just as brutally cold as in February. The wind blowing off Lake Michigan can cut right through a person no matter how many layers of clothing they are wearing. Most Chicagoans joke that if you do not like the weather, wait ten minutes, and it will change. Val had landed at O'Hare Airport mid-morning. The sky was overcast and gray, a typical blustery Chicago day. Trees still remained black and bare from their long winter slumber. It was certainly a culture shock to Val, who grew up in sunny southern California.

The cab ride from O'Hare Airport to downtown Chicago took

nearly an hour. The cabby apologized to Val for the long trip and informed her that the delay was the result of an accident on the Kennedy Expressway. At least the cabbie was listening to a decent radio station, WLS 890 AM radio. WLS played the top 40 songs including, *People Got to be Free* by the Rascals, *Hey Jude* by the Beatles, *Mrs. Robinson* by Simon and Garfunkel, and *Midnight Confessions* by The Grass Roots. Turning off from Randolph onto Michigan Avenue, Val was in awe of the tall buildings and the Chicago skyline.

"First time to Chicago?" the cabby inquired.

"Yes, it is," replied Val with a look of amazement and wonderment. Still astonished at the magnificence of Lakeshore Drive and the surrounding area, Val exited the cab parked in front of the Tribune Tower office building with trepidation.

The Tribune Tower was completed in 1925. Located on North Michigan Avenue in Chicago it was a neo-Gothic building designed by New York architects John Mead Howells and Raymond Hood with buttresses near the top. The building rose more than four hundred fifty feet in the Chicago skyline and had thirty-six floors.

Val, entered the building's lobby, and found the directory. She looked up the law firm of Thornton, Mender and Bigelow and saw, not surprisingly, they were located on one of the top floors of the building, the entire thirty-fifth floor. Val was oblivious to the people milling about in the lobby. The weather outside was still dreary making the building seem more cold and callous than it actually was. As she walked to the elevator, Val was deep in thought as to what she would do when she reached the receptionist.

Val exited the elevator right in the middle of Thornton, Mender and Bigelow's lobby. The receptionist, Marge, sat behind a mahogany desk curved in a semi circle. Marge, a woman in her mid-fifties, was dressed conservatively in a blue suit. Her hair was worn in a beehive style. Telephone lights that blinked on the numerous phone lines did not distract Marge from Val's unexpected appearance. "May I help you?" She asked Val.

"Yes, I'm here to see Mr. Thornton," Val replied in a calm voice.

Marge asked, "Do you have an appointment?"

Val politely responded in a soft voice, "No, but I'm certain he'll see me now."

Marge looked directly at Val ignoring the flashing lights on the switchboard and courteously said, "I doubt that very much. Mr. Thornton never sees anyone without an appointment."

Not intimidated by the receptionist, Val persisted, "Perhaps you should let Mr. Thornton make that decision. My name is Valentina Benjamin."

Without hesitation, Marge picked up the telephone receiver, plugged a cord into the switchboard and stated, "Mr. Thornton, there is a young lady asking to see you without an appointment. She says her name is Valentina Benjamin. What should I tell her?"

Thornton was sitting behind his desk and asked Marge, "What's her name again?"

Marge was a bit taken back at Thornton's response and said, "Valentina Benjamin."

Val could overhear part of the conversation between Marge and Thornton and interrupted with an angelic smile, "Tell him Valentina Benjamin is here and that Sam Shaw sent me."

The receiver fell from Marge's hand as her jaw dropped open and her mouth contorted. Staring blankly at Val, Marge quickly regained her composure and picked up the receiver. She looked like she had just seen a ghost. She then said to Mr. Thornton, "She claims to be sent by Sam Shaw, sir." The next thing Val heard from Marge was a few, "uh huhs" and 'yes, sirs," before being told to have a seat in the lobby and that Mr. Thornton would be with her in a moment.

Marge then called another one of the firm's secretaries and asked her to fill in at the front desk for a few moments. It was clearly visible that Marge was shaken by Val's presence.

Val found a seat on a leather sofa in the reception area. The sofa was positioned so that guests could look out the window at the magnificent lakefront. Within two minutes, a woman in her mid-forties, dressed in a light robin's-egg blue, pastel blouse, and navy blue skirt greeted Val and asked if she'd follow her.

The two moved down the long hallway past several large conference rooms until they came to a corner office. The woman, who Val presumed to be Mr. Thornton's secretary knocked on the office door and said, "Miss Benjamin to see you, sir."

A booming, gruff voice said, "Come in Ms. Benjamin - That will be all Betty."

As Val entered the office, she was greeted warmly by Nathaniel Thornton with a firm handshake. Motioning for her to sit in a black leather chair facing his desk, Thornton stepped back around to his own seat behind a large, two-toned, walnut desk. Thornton's secretary quietly vanished as quickly as she had materialized in the lobby.

The office was elegant, not overly lavish, and modestly decorated. The view, overlooking the Chicago River, was nothing short of breathtaking. Thornton's office was more the size of a small apartment. Complete with a private bathroom and shower, a wet bar, black leather sofa and matching love seat, an art deco glass coffee table, and numerous works of art. Behind Thornton's desk was a matching floor to ceiling walnut bookcase that held volumes of law journals. Off to the side was a credenza with several legal files on top.

Nathaniel Thornton, a native Chicagoan with intense hazel eyes that were magnified by his thick glasses, stood six feet tall. He was professionally dressed in a dark three-piece navy blue pinstripe suit, white shirt, and blue tie. Thornton, a graduate of Northwestern University School of Law was a co-founder of the law firm *Thornton, Mender and Bigelow*. Although he was sixty-five years-old with salt and pepper hair, Thornton was trim, fit, and looked ten years younger than his age.

"So, Ms. Benjamin, what brings you all the way from LA to Chicago?" Thornton asked as he began the conversation. Before letting Val answer, he continued, "May I offer you a drink?" pointing towards the wet bar.

"No thanks," Val replied. "Well, sir, first let me say how sorry I am about attorney Shaw. He's the reason I'm here."

"Really? And why is that?" Thornton inquired not letting on

that he knew everything about the situation.

Val reached into her purse and took out Sam Shaw's business card. She handed it to Thornton. Reaching back into her purse, she withdrew the empty envelope Sam Shaw had given her. She handed the envelope to Thornton watching his face closely for any sign that he knew more than he was letting on. Val noticed Thornton's mouth slightly twitch and quiver as he took the envelope from her hand.

Val said nothing as she handed Thornton the envelope. The silence was broken when he cleared his throat and began to speak, in a melancholy voice, "Sam was a good attorney and a good friend of mine. I never should have sent him to deliver this envelope to you."

Val interrupted, "Did you know my mother?"

With a whimsical laugh and broad smile, Thornton replied, "Yes, I knew both of your mothers."

Val was taken aback by this revelation and asked, "What do you mean you knew both of my mothers?"

"Come now, Ms. Benjamin, let's cut the crap and be blunt with each other. If you have questions about your adoption, just ask. I will tell you what I know and then you can decide what else you want to know. Virginia's been dead for more than two years now." With that said, Thornton laid out in great detail Val's adoption and how he was the attorney involved in the process. He told Val of Virginia's connection with the mob bosses, that Virginia lived in Chicago, and how they had met. He also told Val about the envelope and the contents and what it meant as far as the monetary fortune that waited for her if she could decipher Virginia's riddles.

Thornton's disclosure was an eye-opener for Val. She listened quietly and intently to every word he spoke. After he had finished, Val took out the stock certificates and showed them to him. "Are these part of that fortune?" she asked as she placed the certificates on his desk and pushed them towards him.

Thornton picked up the certificates, quickly flipped through them, and placed them back on his desk. "Yes, as a matter of fact, I'm the one who purchased these certificates on your behalf," he said with a smile. "I was wondering what happened to them," he said, looking at the certificates.

"The dividends from these certificates are placed into an account set up in trust for you in your name. It has been accumulating a lot of money. These certificates are only a small part of what Virginia hid for you." Thornton added, "I think you should leave these here with me for safe keeping. I'll add them to your portfolio."

Val did not immediately understand what Thornton just revealed to her. Her head was swimming with a lot of emotion and a lot of questions. "What do you mean you'll add them to my portfolio?" she asked.

"You have a modest investment portfolio to which I'm the Trustee," Thornton replied. "She told me to manage the dividends, but she wanted to keep the certificates."

Val asked Thornton, "What happened after Virginia died?"

Thornton said nonchalantly, "No one in the mafia had sympathy for her especially when she began telling reporters about her, secret diary that had been safely tucked away in a safe deposit box in

Chicago. She hinted that the diary named gangsters as well as some highly placed government officials. She called the diary her 'insurance'."

"Virginia was found dead about two years ago on March 24, 1966, near a brook in Koppl, Austria. The papers reported her death was a suicide. Those who really knew her believed that she was murdered. She was only forty-nine. On the day of Virginia's death, Joe Epstein and a friend went to the bank to retrieve Virginia's diary. No one knew about this envelope, however, or its contents."

He noticed Val's bewilderment and suggested they continue their conversation at another time. Val nodded her head yes, simply stood up, and said, "Thank you for your time, Mr. Thornton, and the information. May I ask question before I go, "what do you know about Mickey Cohen?"

Thornton said in a monotone voice, "He isn't to be trusted."

Val regained her composure and before she left Thornton's office, she asked, "Sorry Mr. Thornton, one more question, but whatever happened to my Uncle Chick?"

Thornton smiled, looked at Val with a sympathetic look hearing her refer to Chick Hill as "uncle" and said, "I don't know. I never followed his whereabouts and Virginia made it clear to me that nothing was to be discussed about our business relationship with anyone, not even her brother Chick. So there was no real reason for me to try to keep in contact with him. I did hear he had some legal issues, but I never met Chick and he never tried to contact me. The only thing I knew about Chick was that he introduced Virginia to your parents,

Martha and Stewart."

With that, said, Val exited Thornton's office with the envelope but left the stock certificates on his desk.

Upon exiting Thornton's office, attorney Michael Caldwell passed her in the hallway. Knocking on Thornton's door, Caldwell waited a moment for Thornton to acknowledge his presence and grant him permission to enter. "Was that Valentina Benjamin?" he asked.

Thornton answered, "Yes."

It was now mid-afternoon, and the weather turned delightful, a balmy sixty-eight degrees, sunny, with blue skies and no wind. As Val stepped outside the Tribune Tower, she collected her thoughts as to her next move. Thornton had given her a great deal of information about her biological mother, Virginia Hill, though little had been said about her biological father, Benjamin Siegel.

Walking down Michigan Avenue towards Ohio Street, Val turned west on Ohio toward Wabash Avenue. As she walked, she realized she was hungry. She had not eaten anything all day. As she approached Wabash, she noticed Pizzeria Uno, a Chicago landmark.

Pizzeria Uno was founded in 1943 by Ike Sewell. Sewell served a deep dish pizza unlike any that had been served before. It had a buttery 'out-of-this-world' crust with a tall edge like a fruit pie. When people tasted it, they wanted more, and lines had been forming ever since to get into the restaurant. Fortunately for Val, it was already 2:30 p.m. and the lunch crowd had diminished. She was seated immediately.

After finishing lunch, Val decided to head back to LA that same evening. "Do you have a pay phone I can use?" she asked the waitress.

"Yes, around the corner over there," the waitress responded as she pointed Val in the right direction. Val called Artimis.

The operator chimed in, "Please deposit one dollar fifty cents to complete this call." Val deposited the coins and then heard, "Hello."

"Hey, it's Val. I'm catching the 6 p.m. flight back to LA tonight. Can you pick me up at the airport?"

Artimis, glad to hear her voice, said, "Of course I can. What did you find out?" Val replied, "I'll tell you when I see you later. I'm arriving at nine-thirty p.m. on United Airlines flight 489."

Artimis jotted the flight information down on a piece of paper as he said, "Got it! See you tonight."

Upon completing her phone call to Artimis, Val strolled around downtown Chicago and did some window shopping. She stopped in at Marshall Field & Company on State Street and was astounded by the size of the store.

Originally started in the 1860's, Marshall Field's became a Chicago landmark after the Great Chicago Fire. In 1906, Marshall Field & Co. continued the rebuilding and transformation of its store by tearing down the 1879 structure and constructing the South State Street building with a continuation of the 1902 façade. When the store opened in September 1907, it included a Tiffany Ceiling that was both the first and largest ceiling ever built in Favrile glass, containing over one point six million pieces.

Val was overwhelmed and amazed with its façade and structure but had had enough for one day. She exited the store and caught a cab back to O'Hare Airport. Not in the mood for conversation with the cab driver, she closed her eyes and listened to the music being played on the radio: *Those were the Days* by Mary Hopkin. The next song was *Love Child* by Diana Ross and the Supremes, and Val, while listening to the music, was thinking how ironic it was for those two songs to be playing back to back on the radio. She was half asleep in the back of the cab when they arrived at O'Hare International Airport.

Chapter 19

Within fifteen minutes of Val departing from Thornton's office in Chicago, Michael Caldwell placed a call to Mickey Cohen. Caldwell was dressed in a pinstripe navy blue suit, a soft powder blue shirt, and a funky tie-dye tie. He wore black penny loafers and black argyle socks. Except for the tie, he was dressed conservatively. He placed his horn-rimmed glasses on the walnut-finished desk as he waited for Mickey to answer the phone.

"Hello Mickey," Caldwell said. "Valentina Benjamin just left Thornton's office a few minutes ago." Mickey listened carefully as Caldwell filled him in on Val's visit. "No, I'm not certain what was said or why she was here."

Mickey asked Caldwell if he found out anything more about the El Rancho Mirage. Caldwell had been doing a title search and a search for who had been paid by the insurance company, as Mickey requested. Caldwell put on his horn-rimmed glasses, pulled out a file from his desk drawer and he reported to Mickey, "El Rancho Vegas was a hotel and casino on the Las Vegas Strip owned by Joe Drown. It was located on the southwest corner of Las Vegas Boulevard and Sahara, and opened on April 3, 1941. On June 17, 1960, while Harry James and Betty Grable were performing a late show on stage, the hotel was destroyed by fire. There was no evidence as to what caused the fire and there were no deaths or injuries."

Mickey listened closely as Caldwell continued his detailed report, "In December 1944, William Wilkerson leased the Casino for six months for fifty thousand dollars. He would later go on to build the Flamingo Hotel, but you already knew that. In September 1945, El Rancho Vegas was sold for one point five million to a Los Angeles businessman, Walter Guzzardi. The casino went through several changes of ownership before Beldon Katleman, who received a share of ownership upon the death of his uncle, Jake Katleman, in 1947, bought out the remaining shareholders and became the proprietor of record. Despite Katleman's vow to rebuild the El Rancho Vegas after the fire, he never did. As far as I can determine, Katleman kept the insurance money for himself."

Mickey interrupted, "Any records with Joe's name on a deed to the El Rancho?" he asked.

"No sir, none that were recorded."

Mickey said, "Thanks for the information, keep me posted if anything turns up with Thornton," and hung up the phone.

Mickey was sitting at his desk at the Flamingo holding a fat Arturo Fuente cigar. He was in deep thought after his conversation with Caldwell and the cigar smoke circled over his head and hung in the air.

When the cigar was about halfway smoked, Mickey crushed the lit end into a heavy, gray marble ashtray and put it out. He was still mulling over what Caldwell told him about Valentina being in Chicago. Mickey was not pleased.

Chapter 20

The special effects director's office was partially restored as Artimis sat at his desk working on the schematics of his new movie assignment. Deep in thought, he failed to hear Agent Atwood knock at the door. After a brief moment, Agent Atwood, not a person usually kept waiting, coughed loudly. Startled, Artimis jumped what seemed to be about three feet in the air, but in reality, it was just a few inches. His heart pounded as he turned to see Atwood smiling. "Sorry, didn't mean to scare you like that. But I did knock."

"I'm sure you did," Artimis said as he stood to greet Atwood.

Agent Atwood extended his hand to shake Artimis'. "Agent Atwood, FBI. You must be Artimis Sylver."

"That's right," Artimis replied, withdrawing his hand after the handshake.

"I brought you a souvenir," Atwood said holding out a piece of round lead in his right hand. "It's one of the slugs retrieved from your office wall. I took it from the evidence room since they have more than enough for the case. Care to fill me in on what this is all about?"

Artimis, being more suspicious and cautious after the past few weeks, looked at Atwood with a wary eye.

"Agent Atwood, let me see your badge," Artimis responded. Atwood showed his badge to Artimis and made certain to leave it out long enough for Artimis to get a good look at it. "Fine," said Artimis as he took the slug from Atwood's right hand. Artimis held the slug up close to his face so that he could examine it more carefully.

"Have a seat, Agent Atwood," Artimis said as he motioned to a chair next to his.

"So, here's the deal," Atwood started. "You cooperate and you and your girlfriend, Valentina, stay out of jail. Otherwise, I put you both away for a very long time. By the way, where is Ms. Benjamin?"

Artimis did not like the tone of Atwood's voice, looked at him and replied, "Val's at my apartment. Why the hardball questions Agent Atwood?"

Atwood placed the tips of his fingers together like a steeple, as if praying, smiled, and said, "National security, you might say." He leaned forward then. "I'll tell you the little I know so far, and you fill in the blanks. An attorney from Chicago named Sam Shaw flew to LA to deliver an envelope to Valentina Benjamin right here in this office. What did Mr. Shaw say to Valentina when he gave her the envelope?"

Artimis listened intently to Atwood's question and responded, "Nothing much. Just that the envelope had been in his law firm's possession for a long time, then he checked the tattoo on the back of her left shoulder to make sure it matched the image on the envelope. He left saying, 'have a nice life'. Before Val had a chance to open the envelope, we heard an explosion and went outside to see what had happened. That's when the bullets started flying. Afterwards, when the police cars showed up, we left and went to Val's apartment. Her apartment was ransacked so we cleaned up the place before we left and went to my place. That's where she opened the envelope."

"What was in the envelope," Atwood interrupted.

Artimis decided not to give Atwood too many details and said, "A letter, some photos, and some playing cards from different casinos." Artimis intentionally failed to mention the thirty thousand dollars as he continued, "The letter said something to the effect that her mother would be long gone by the time she read it. That shocked Val because she had just spoken to her mother the week before."

Atwood continued his informal interrogation and asked, "What happened next?"

Artimis answered, "Well, Val was real upset, so we drove to her parents' home to see her mom. That's when Val learned she was adopted and that her biological parents were Bugsy Siegel and Virginia Hill." He then said "You don't really expect me to believe this has anything to with national security, do you? That's all I know about Sam Shaw, anyway, so what's this really about?"

Atwood stayed relaxed and calmly said to Artimis, "Okay, kid, you've been upfront with me so far so here's the skinny. Mickey Cohen called me and said to back off the investigation. Cohen said it was Tony Ionnatti who blew Shaw to bits and that I could find Ionnatti's body buried in a hole in the desert near a burnt out Lincoln Town Car. You know anything about that?"

Artimis lied and stated he had no knowledge of what Atwood was talking about.

Atwood pressed on, "So, that raises more questions than answers. For instance, why was Shaw killed by Ionnati and who hired Ionnati to kill Shaw. Then who killed Ionnati and why? Everything leads back to a crime boss in Chicago named Jordan Hamilton."

Artimis raised an eyebrow hearing at Hamilton's name. Artimis' expression did not go unnoticed by Atwood. "Seems I struck a nerve mentioning Hamilton's name, eh?"

Before Artimis could respond, Val walked through the office door.

"Hello sweetie," she said.

Artimis stood up from his chair and said, "Hey Val, this is FBI Agent Atwood - he's investigating the death of Sam Shaw."

Atwood rose from his chair and extended his right hand to Val. "Hello Ms. Benjamin, I have a few questions for you, if I may."

Val was surprised to see Agent Atwood and asked, "Certainly, how can I help, Agent Atwood?"

Atwood re-stated what he had told Artimis - that he was investigating the murder of attorney Sam Shaw. "As I explained to Mr. Sylver here, you two can cooperate with me or you both can end up in jail."

Val sat down at her desk and said, "Fine, what do you want to know?" Artimis tensed up then. He hoped Agent Atwood didn't ask Val what was in the envelope.

Atwood continued his questioning, "What were you doing in Vegas the past few days? And don't tell me you were there gambling. I already know that Mickey Cohen was keeping you under his watch."

Val was not about to divulge too much information about what she was doing in Vegas but said politely, "Agent Atwood, first, I have no idea why Sam Shaw was murdered. He said he was here to deliver an envelope to me as part of his assignment for his law firm." Val reached into her purse and pulled out Shaw's business card, "Here's the card he gave me."

Val handed the card to Atwood who examined it and then asked, "May I keep this?"

Val no longer needed the card and said, "Of course." She continued, "The content of the envelope is my personal property and really none of your business. Unless you have a search warrant or can prove it has something to do with Mr. Shaw's murder, it is a private matter. Artimis and I went to Vegas because I learned that my biological parents were Bugsy Siegel and Virginia Hill and I wanted to find out some more information about them and what Virginia wrote in a letter to me that was in the envelope."

Atwood shrugged his shoulders, sat with hands together, again as if praying, and asked, "So, what happened with the Lincoln?" Val was flabbergasted at Atwood's question. Atwood, however, continued, "Come on, Val, Mickey Cohen called me and said Tony Iannotti was the body that was buried in the desert and that Iannotti killed Shaw. We have the body and know Iannotti was shot in the head at close range. You want to tell me what happened?"

Val quit pretending and said, "Yeah, I'll tell you what happened. These two guys started tailing us from Caesars Palace after we finished lunch. We tried to lose them with some gimmicks Artimis had installed into my Mustang. I thought for sure they were going to kill us. We were able to cause them to lose control of their car. That's all I'm saying about the matter without an attorney being present. If you have any more questions, go talk to Jordan Hamilton in Chicago. Iannotti and Jerry worked for him. But if you want my opinion, I don't think Iannotti killed Shaw. Now please leave."

Atwood looked at Val with intensity and said, "You're very good Miss Benjamin. You're right about Iannotti not killing Shaw. And I'm fairly certain Iannotti wasn't the person shooting at you. The pattern of the bullet holes on the outside of your door indicates whoever was shooting at you intentionally missed. However, the bomb that killed Shaw was professionally done. I'll keep in touch."

Atwood arose from the chair, grinned, and said, "Thank you. I appreciate the information and your cooperation." Atwood left the office.

Once Atwood was gone, Val asked Artimis, "What the hell is that all about? Why is the FBI involved?"

Artimis said, "Atwood gave some lame reason that it involved national security. He knew I wasn't buying it. So, what did you find out in Chicago?"

Val was coy about her answer, "Only that Mr. Nathaniel Thornton was Virginia's attorney, and he handled my adoption paperwork for her."

Artimis pressed the issue, "Did he say anything about the cards or what was in the envelope?"

Val curtly responded, "Nope, and I didn't ask. He did know about the stock certificates." Val changed the subject by stating, "Hey, we better get some work done before we both get fired."

Artimis grinned and flashed one of his dazzling smiles at Val, "Honestly? You're joking, right? You got half a million dollars in stock certificates, clues that will lead you to more money, and you're worried about *this job*?"

Val was not amused and said, "Yeah, I'm not touching the money yet, and I like what we do here. So, yeah, I want to keep my job. Let's just let things cool down a bit, and, in a few weeks, we'll head back to Vegas."

Artimis was surprised with Val's thinking but said, "Fine, we'll do it your way. But I still want to figure out the rest of the clues on the two remaining cards."

Chapter 21

A few weeks passed and Val and Artimis had not heard anything from anyone. All was quiet. Val was happy to be back in L.A., working on the next MGM film, *Where Were You When the Lights Went Out* staring Doris Day, Lola Albright, Patrick O'Neal, and Robert Morse. Artimis and Val had just finished enjoying a celebratory dinner at the Ambassador Hotel when they decided stop in at the Cocoanut Grove nightclub. Artimis was wearing dressy, bell-bottomed slacks with a white silk shirt that was unbuttoned at the top to show his chest and a gold peace medallion. Val was wearing a bright red mini dress with a hemline well above the thighs and white go-go boots.

The Ambassador Hotel formally opened on January 1, 1921. It was located on Wilshire Boulevard in the center of Los Angeles.

For decades, the hotel's famed Cocoanut Grove nightclub hosted well-known entertainers, such as Frank Sinatra, Barbara Streisand, Judy Garland, Lena Horne, Bing Crosby, and many others. In addition to the nightclub, the hotel was a frequent site for movie, music video, and television filming. *The Graduate* was filmed at the Ambassador Hotel, renamed for that movie the Taft Hotel.

As they walked through the lobby, Artimis noticed a campaign for Robert F. Kennedy. Suddenly, a light bulb went off in his head. "Hey Val, what was it Peter Lawford said to you about saying hi to Bobby?"

Val was not sure where Artimis was going with the question since they had not spent too much time thinking about the cards and Virginia Hill. "I don't know, just that it seemed an odd thing for him to say."

Artimis took Val's hand and said, "Come on, let's look at the clue on the Queen of Spades."

As they drove back to Val's apartment, Artimis asked her if she remembered what was written on the Queen of Spades. Val said she did not remember. When they arrived at Val's apartment, she went into her bedroom and lifted a corner of the green shag carpeting in the closet. She had hidden both envelopes and their content there for safe keeping. She pulled out the envelope given to her by Shaw and joined Artimis in the living room. Val dumped the contents of the envelope onto the coffee table and picked up the Queen of Spades card.

Val looked at the card from the Dunes and read what was written on it out loud, "Seek out the man who lives in the shadow of another, for he has a gift from me to you. Bobby is a friend I can trust like no other."

Artimis flipped through the photos until he found the photo of Virginia sitting with Marilyn Monroe and John Kennedy. "Ah ha," he said as he held up the photo to show Val. "Look Val, the menu on the table is from the Dunes Casino. This photo was taken at the Dunes with Virginia, John Kennedy and Marilyn Monroe. I'll wager anything that Bobby is Bobby Kennedy."

Val looked at the photo and agreed. "That makes perfect sense. Now all we have to do is figure out a way to meet with Bobby Kennedy during a presidential race," she said sarcastically.

Val paced the floor, wearing a path in the green shag carpeting. As she paced, she thought out loud, "Who can we trust to connect us with Bobby Kennedy? Christ, he's running for President. No way are we going to be able to get past his bodyguards and security."

Artimis was listening to Val think out loud and said, "What about Mickey?"

Val quickly shot him down. "Na, Thornton said he can't be trusted. Besides, he's the one who told the FBI about our little incident in the desert. I'm still not sure why he called Atwood."

Artimis then suggested Jordan Hamilton or Thornton. Again, Val shot him down. She continued to think and said, "Who can connect us with Bobby that doesn't have a hidden agenda in this mess?" A moment later it came to her, "I got it!" she said.

Artimis startled, looked at Val and said, "Okay, who?"

Val smiled, "Agent Atwood." Artimis was stunned at the thought of calling Agent Atwood and said, "Are you out of your frickin' mind? Why bring in the FBI?"

Val kissed Artimis on the cheek, "Look, big dummy, he wants answers about Shaw, and he came up with the lame excuse that it was about national security. It makes perfect sense to tell him we need to talk to Bobby because of national security. I'm sure he'll play along."

Val picked up the phone and called Atwood. "Hello, Agent Atwood, this is Valentina Benjamin. Sir, I need a favor from you."

Atwood was surprised by the phone call. "Really?" he said. "What kind of favor are we talking about?"

Val was straight upfront with Atwood, and said, "I need to meet with Bobby Kennedy."

Atwood listened closely to Val and said, "Robert Kennedy, the presidential candidate?"

Val said, "Yes, that Robert Kennedy; it's a matter of national security." Atwood was amused with Val's dig about needing to meet with Robert Kennedy because it was a matter of national security.

"Does this have anything to do with Shaw's murder?

Val responded, "Yes, sir, it does." Atwood chuckled to himself, "Okay, Ms. Benjamin, let me see what I can do." Val thanked Atwood as they each hung up, smiling.

Chapter 22

True to his word, Agent Atwood made some telephone calls and was successful in arranging a meeting between Val and presidential candidate Robert Kennedy.

Atwood informed Val that her meeting with Kennedy was scheduled to take place in San Francisco at the Fairmont Hotel. The Hotel sat atop Nob Hill, affording breathtaking views of the city and bay with easy access to the Financial District, Union Square, and Fisherman's Wharf.

In November 1961, the Fairmont opened a twenty-three-story tower, designed by Mario Gaidano. The newly added tower had San Francisco's first glass elevator that went to the Crown Room at the top of the building.

Agent Atwood called in several favors to arrange for Val and Artimis to meet with Robert F. Kennedy. Security was already tight, and Secret Service was on high-alert. The Presidential campaign was a close race. There was violence in the air, especially after King's assassination earlier in April. Still, Atwood was able to arrange the meeting.

Val and Artimis flew to San Francisco and arrived at the Fairmont at approximately six p.m. The San Francisco evening was cold, dark, overcast, and gloomy as the fog rolled into the Bay Area. They first went to the front desk and asked for Mr. Goodwin. Val was given specific instructions by Atwood that she was to ask for Mr. Goodwin and he would ensure that she was taken to see Bobby Kennedy. The front desk clerk rang to Mr. Goodwin's room and informed him that his guest had arrived.

Goodwin met Val and Artimis in the hotel lobby. After exchanging pleasantries and greetings, Artimis and Val were searched by security. After being cleared, Goodwin escorted the two to a meeting room on the hotel's sixth floor. Kennedy was already waiting in the room when they arrived.

"Pleased to meet you, Mr. Kennedy," Val said, grasping Kennedy's hand with her own. Her beam of excitement radiated, having been personally introduced to Bobby Kennedy. Although immaculately dressed, he appeared tired from hours of campaigning.

He greeted Val and shook Artimis's hand. Four men, presumably body guards, stood by watching every move that Val and Artimis made.

The room was art-deco style with ornate murals. Not having much time Kennedy handed Val a manila envelope with the marking of the Florentine "F" and card suits surrounding it on the outside. The envelope was sealed.

"This is what you came for," he said as he handed it to Val. He said that he received the envelope from Virginia in what he described as a chance meeting. In hindsight, Kennedy was not so certain that it was an accident he met Virginia.

As Attorney General, Kennedy pursued a relentless crusade against organized crime and the mafia. Sometimes he disagreed with J. Edgar Hoover regarding strategies. Convictions against organized crime figures rose by eight hundred percent during his term as Attorney General.

It was a surprise when Virginia Hill, a person with known connections to the mob, met with Kennedy and gave him the envelope to hold for her. Virginia's message to Bobby was very simple, "Keep this for the rightful owner who claims it. You'll know who she is when she asks for it." Kennedy placed the envelope in his safe and because of his hectic schedule, did not give it much thought. He had completely forgotten about the envelope until he received a phone call from Agent Atwood asking him to meet with Valentina. Once Kennedy learned from Atwood that Valentina was Virginia's biological daughter, he knew the envelope was meant for her.

Val immediately tore open the envelope in front of Kennedy and his bodyguards. As a precaution, the bodyguards pulled their weapons, not knowing what was inside the envelope. The envelope contained a framed photo of Virginia Hill, Marilyn Monroe, and John F. Kennedy posing together. There was no note or any other message with the photo. Kennedy shook his head in amazement when he realized the photo was the only thing in the envelope. The bodyguards lowered their weapons when they saw there was no danger. His business with Val finished, Robert Kennedy said his goodbyes and left the room with the bodyguards.

Val held the picture in her hand and stood dumbfounded as Artimis gazed over her left shoulder to look at the photo. "That's it?" Artimis exclaimed. "This is what all the fuss was about? Another photo?"

Val put it back inside the envelope and said, "There's gotta be more. But let's not discuss it here."

Val and Artimis immediately left The Fairmont and went to the airport to catch the next flight back to L.A.

Early the next morning the telephone in Val's apartment rang. Val picked up the receiver and said, "Hello." On the other end of the line was Agent Atwood. In a cheerful voice, he said, "Good morning, Ms. Benjamin. Did you get what you wanted from Mr. Kennedy?" Still half asleep Val answered, "Sorta."

Atwood then asked, "What was it?"

Val was starting to wake up and said, "It was a framed photo of John Kennedy, Marilyn Monroe and Virginia Hill. That was it. Even Bobby seemed perplexed that he was asked by Virginia to keep it safe for me. I'm sorry Agent Atwood, but I don't know how this is related to Sam Shaw's death. If I come up with anything else, I'll call you."

Atwood said, "Okay, Ms. Benjamin, keep in touch." With that, she hung up the phone and got ready for work.

Shortly after Val arrived at her office, Artimis came in with two cups of coffee and donuts. "Hey Val, did you bring that photo with you today?" he asked.

Val said, "No. But don't worry; it's in a safe place. Thanks for the coffee and donuts."

A few minutes later, the office phone rang. Artimis answered. "It's for you," he said, handing the phone to Val.

She took the phone and said, "Hello, this is Val Benjamin."

Mickey Cohen said, "Hi Val, Mickey Cohen. I understand you got something from Bobby Kennedy last night."

Val was annoyed and agitated that Cohen knew about her

secret meeting with Kennedy and answered, "Yeah, what about it?"

Mickey ignored the tone of her answer and asked, "What did he give you?"

In a calmer voice, Val answered, "Just a framed photo of John Kennedy, Marilyn Monroe and Virginia Hill. Actually, I think it's the exact photo that was in the envelope Sam Shaw gave me."

Mickey pressed the issue, "Anything else?"

Val responded, "Nope, just a picture. No note, nothing. Even Robert Kennedy was surprised about all the fuss."

Mickey thought there was more than what Val was saying, "All right, can you bring it out to me in Vegas for me to look at?" he asked.

Val took a pause, and then replied, "Sure, I'll let you know when Artimis and I can get out there. It will be a few days."

Mickey said, "I'll look forward to seeing you both again," as he hung up the phone.

A few days later Artimis and Val flew back to Vegas to see Mickey. Val was still without her beloved Mustang. For the most part, she was driving Artimis' Corvette when she was not hanging around with him. It was approximately one p.m. when they went to check in at the front desk. They were told by the clerk that their room was ready. He handed a note to Val. The note was from Mickey, requesting that she call him immediately upon their arrival.

Once Val and Artimis were situated in their room, Val called Mickey to let him know they were at the casino. Mickey asked Val to meet him in his office and to bring the framed photo. A few minutes later, Val and Artimis headed to Mickey's office.

Val knocked on Mickey's door and waited for him to answer. Mickey opened the door and greeted Val and Artimis with a warm welcome, "Hello, you two come on in." Mickey was all smiles as he waited a few moments before asking Val for the photo. Before Mickey had a chance to ask for the photo, however, Val took it out of her purse and handed it to him. Mickey took the photo and examined it carefully.

Mickey became teary eyed and a little emotional seeing the photo of the three people. Val, watching Mickey closely, asked him, "So what's significant about this picture?"

Mickey asked Val if she had made a deal with Hamilton. Val and Artimis both smiled and Val said in a playful voice, "You damn well know about my meeting with Hamilton." But how did you know about my tattoo and where I lived?"

Mickey, tired of keeping his secret for all of these years, finally told Val about his life with Virginia and Bugsy Siegel. Val and Artimis listen intently as Mickey told them how Virginia gave him enough money to retire, and Bugsy made sure he had a lifetime job at the Flamingo by giving him part ownership of the casino. Mickey's official job title was "Curator." Mickey had enough dirt on the other partners to ensure nobody would bother him.

Mickey laughed and said how ironic it was that her biological father's name was Benjamin and that she was adopted by parents with the last name of Benjamin.

Once Mickey was done answering Val's questions and telling her about his story, he turned the frame over and removed the back.

Behind the photo was the deed to the El Rancho Casino. Examining the deed closer, Mickey saw that it was signed by Joseph Kennedy transferring ownership to Frank Costello.

Handing the deed to Val he said, "Here, this is what Hamilton is looking for. Mickey replaced the back of the frame and handed it and the deed to Val. She took the deed and frame from Mickey, removed the back of the frame, and replaced the deed.

"Looks like I'll be making another trip to Chicago," Val said.

Mickey picked up on her comment and asked, "When were you in Chicago?" even though he was fully aware of her visit to Thornton's office a few weeks earlier. Mickey was testing Val.

Val responded, "A few weeks ago. I met with Nathaniel Thornton." She grinned wickedly, flashed a smile that revealed her perfectly white teeth and said, "But you probably already knew that."

Mickey did not respond. He just shook his head knowing that she was one smart cookie.

As Val and Artimis departed Mickey's office, Mickey said, "Give my regards to Jordan."

Val said, "Will do," as she headed out the door.

She and Artimis were inside the elevator heading back to their room when Artimis spoke up. "Did that seem to go too easy or am I missing something?"

Val turned to Artimis, smiled and said, "Yeah, Mickey was too calm, and him giving that deed back so fast, seems strange.

Artimis said, "We'd better be extra careful. I don't like the way things are playing out." Val agreed as they exited the elevator.

Mickey wasted no time in calling Jordan Hamilton to inform him that the deed was found, "Jordan, Mickey Cohen. The girl's got the deed. It appears Robert Kennedy had the deed the entire time and didn't know it."

Hamilton asked, "Where is it now?"

Mickey answered, "The deed was in the inside of a framed photo Virginia gave to Bobby. Apparently, Virginia instructed Bobby to hold onto the envelope that contained the photo until the rightful person came to claim it. She met Bobby in San Francisco a few days ago, and Bobby gave her the envelope. Nothing else inside the envelope just the framed photograph. Val and her friend brought the photo to me. I opened the back, and everyone saw the deed. Val put the deed back inside the frame and left."

Hamilton lost his temper, "You let her go?" he exclaimed

"Of course I did," said Mickey. "She's going to Chicago to deliver it to you in person."

Hamilton settled down and laughed, "So she really believed me when I said we'd be even-steven if she gave me the deed?"

Mickey simply said, "I guess so."

Having ended his conversation with Hamilton, Mickey poured himself a glass of Macallan Highland Single Malt Scotch, lit up a fat Arturo Fuente stogie, and walked over to the window looking out at the Vegas sprawl.

Chapter 23

The brightness of a full moon pierced through a sliver of the curtains and fell on Artimis' face to awaken him from a sound sleep. Val lay curled up next to him sleeping in perfect bliss. He nudged Val to wake her, "Hey, what time is it?" he asked. Val moaned and rubbed her eyes as she woke up.

"How the hell do I know?" she answered. Artimis turned on the lamp next to the bed. He picked up his watch and saw it was only ten p.m. "Hey Val," he said, "It's ten o'clock you wanna go get some dinner and maybe gamble a bit?"

By now, Val was fully awake and said, "Why not? Actually I'm famished."

Val and Artimis quickly took turns showering. Artimis dressed in black dress slacks and pink shirt and wore his peace sign medallion on a long gold rope chain around his neck. Val put on a blue and yellow mini dress and black go-go boots. They decided to stay at the Flamingo and have dinner at its main restaurant.

Each of them ordered a steak, baked potato, and salad for dinner. They shared a bottle of Robert Mondavi Merlot with their meal. Val tenderly held Artimis' hands as he sat across the table. Few words were spoken between the two as they enjoyed a quiet meal together. After dinner, Val and Artimis made their way to a craps table.

Artimis pulled out five hundred dollars from a money clip he kept in his front pocket and laid it on the craps table layout. The dealer picked up the five one-hundred dollar bills, and put them in front of the box-man, who counted out the money. After laying the cash on the layout for the eye-in-the-sky to see, he put it into the drop box. The dealer pushed five hundred dollars in chips to Artimis. As Val watched the money disappear into the box, her only thought was, "Is this the casino's way of telling players to say good-bye to their money?" Artimis picked up the stack of chips and placed them in the rack in front of him.

The stickman pushed the dice to a lady at the far end of the table. He called out, "Coming out, new shooter." Standing next to the shooter was a gentleman dressed in a dark suit, white shirt, and wide colorful tie. The lady picked up the dice and tossed them to the other end of the table where Val and Artimis stood. Artimis had placed a twenty-five dollar chip on the Pass Line. As the dice danced on the green felt, rolled around and finally stopped, the stickman called out, "Seven, front line winner." After the players had been paid, the stickman pushed the dice once again to the lady.

In the background of the casino was a commotion of loud, intricate, and convoluted noise. The one-arm bandits dropped silver dollar coins into the metallic tray with clings and clatter. Beautiful cocktail waitresses skimpily clad in their outfits called out, "Cocktails, cigarettes, cigars," to the patrons as they walked around the casino floor. The roulette wheel spun in silent motion as the ball whirled around the side until finally landing on a number. Cards were shuffled at the blackjack tables.

Back at the craps table, the lady tossed the dice. As they spun around and bounced back off the opposite wall, the stickperson called out, "Six, mark the point, the point is six – mark it."

Artimis threw in chips to cover the hard-way numbers. He also placed odds behind his Pass Line bet and tossed in another fifty-five dollars to place the five and eight. The dice were again rolled and a pair of fours appeared. "Hard eight," the stickperson called out to an excited crowd at the table.

Each time the lady tossed the dice and Artimis won, he pressed his bets. The time passed quickly. Val was having a good time watching Artimis continue to play; he was having exceptional luck and his winnings were accumulating.

Forty-five minutes later, the lady was still the shooter. The craps table was packed two-players deep as people tried to get in on the action. Artimis had increased his bets to two hundred fifty and three hundred on each number including the hard-way numbers. He had also made some one hundred dollar bets on the proposition numbers. The large bets caught the pit boss' attention. He walked over to Artimis, looked at him and said, "Mr. Sylver, you seem to be doing very well tonight."

Artimis, smiled back and replied, "Yeah, who would have thought I could get so lucky," as he winked at Val. "Is there a problem?"

The pit boss then said, "No, no problem." With that Artimis had a feeling and asked the dealer to take down all his bets.

The dealer removed Artimis's bets from the table and pushed the chips toward him. The stick person impatiently waited as Artimis picked up his chips and placed them in his rack. The stick person pushed the dice to the shooter. The next roll was a seven out. The dealer called, "Seven-out, line away." The table erupted with a loud round of applause for the shooter who blushed. The dealers rapidly removed all of the losing bets. Once the commotion died down, Artimis calmly placed all of his chips on the table and said to the dealer, "Color out."

The dealer moved the large stacks of chips to the center where he counted the chips in front of the box man. The box man, with the pit boss standing right behind him and looking over his shoulder, finished counting the chips, and called out, "Thirty-five thousand, five-hundred and ten dollars." The box-man pushed seven five-thousand, bright yellow chips, a five-hundred dollar purple chip and two five dollar red chips to the dealer. The dealer moved the stack of chips to Artimis. As he picked them up, he tossed the purple five-hundred dollar chip to the dealer and said, "For the boys. Thanks, gents." Artimis and Val immediately left the table and headed straight to the cashier's cage.

Val walked next to Artimis holding his right arm tightly. "I'm impressed," she said as she snuggled a little closer. After the cashier finished counting out thirty-five thousand, five-hundred and ten dollars to Artimis, Artimis asked for an envelope to hold the cash. "Sorry sir, but we don't have an envelope," she said with a pleasant smile.

Artimis took the cash from the counter and handed it to Val, "Here, put this in your purse." Val beamed as Artimis handed her the cash.

Val looked at Artimis and said, "What now, hot shot?" Artimis was clever but he knew he had been lucky at the craps table, "My suggestion is we pack our things and fly back to L.A. tonight. Besides, I'm not comfortable that the pit boss singled me out when a lot of the other players were winning big, too."

Val smiled. "I'm with you. Let's blow this joint and get the hell out of town!"

Chapter 24

A few days later, Artimis and Val flew to Chicago to meet Jordan Hamilton. It was a gorgeous day in Chicago when Artimis and Val arrived at Jordan Hamilton's office. The sky was a clear blue and the temperature was a perfect seventy-eight degree, a rarity for Chicago. Having already been to the Windy City, Val was not as impressed as Artimis. It was Artimis' first visit to the third largest city in the U.S.

Val and Artimis were escorted into Hamilton's office by his receptionist. Three of Hamilton's bodyguards were milling about when the two entered the room.

Val removed the photo Kennedy had given her from her purse and handed it to Jordan without saying a word. The bodyguards watched intensely what was happening between Val and their boss. Jordan took the photo from Val and asked, "What's this?"

Val replied, "This is why Sam Shaw was murdered."

Hamilton looked at the photo and said, "Really? This is just a photo of John Kennedy, Marilyn Monroe and Virginia Hill. What could possibly be in this photo worth killing for?"

Val was not amused with Hamilton's game of playing stupid. She was direct and to the point, "Look Hamilton, I'm tired of your bullshit. You know damn well that what you want is behind the photo. I have no doubt your buddy Mickey Cohen called you the minute we left his office."

Hamilton feigned ignorance and said, "Hey, lady, put a muzzle on it, or I'll shut you up myself."

Val looked at him with cold steely eyes and calmly and said

nothing.

Hamilton smiled and removed the back of the frame where he found the deed. Holding it up, he took out his cigarette lighter from his right pants' pocket and lit the document. As the deed went up in flames, he dropped it in a nearby wastebasket. Artimis and Val stood unmoved by Hamilton's action.

Val looked on with a puzzled expression and said, "Why the hell did you do that?"

What? No reaction to my burning the deed?" Hamilton asked staring straight at Artimis. Artimis looked at Val, grinned, and turned to Hamilton, saying, "Why should we care what you do with it? We have copies . . . lots and lots of copies. So, if anything happens to either one of us, we have people who have been instructed to release those copies to the press."

Hamilton's smugness was quickly erased upon hearing what Artimis had to say. "Get the hell out of my office!" he yelled.

Before turning to leave, Val stared Hamilton down and said in a menacing voice, "You'd better keep your word and leave us alone."

Hamilton shouted back, "Get out!"

Artimis and Val made a hasty exit.

* * *

Joe sat in his office at his home in Hyannis Port, Massachusetts. He was in a foul mood from dealing with a bout of   aphasia. His assistant, Jack Brodsky, was watching as Joe scribbled out a message. Joe worked behind the scenes to continue building the financial and political fortunes of his family after his son, John was assassinated.

After a disabling stroke in December 1961, Joe was diagnosed with aphasia and lost all power of speech. He remained mentally intact however and retained full cognitive abilities even though he was confined to a wheelchair.

Jack Brodsky had a muscular build, a square jaw, sandy brown hair and dazzling hazel eyes. He was a college football star at Penn State who graduated from the University Of Virginia School Of Law. Brodsky obtained the position as assistant to Joe as a favor for Bobby Kennedy who had been a classmate of his at law school.

Joe wrote on his message, "Get Hamilton on the phone. I want to know if he's has that document yet."

Brodsky got Hamilton on the phone.

Hamilton was assured him that he had gotten the deed back from the girl, "But Jack, tell Joe that Virginia gave the deed back to him years ago. It was with Bobby." Brodsky was relaying the conversation to Joe as Joe quickly wrote his thoughts back to him on a yellow legal pad.

Brodsky asked, "Joe wants to know what you're talking about. Bobby never had the deed and never knew about the deed."

Hamilton remained calm as he told Brodsky, "Yeah, tell Joe that Bobby had it, but he just didn't know it. You know Virginia was a clever, sneaky bitch. She put the deed behind a photo in a picture frame and asked Bobby to hold it until the rightful owner claimed it."

Brodsky told Joe what Hamilton said. Joe furiously wrote, "What happened to Virginia's daughter?"

Hamilton responded, "She and her boyfriend left my office

about ten minutes ago."

"Okay, okay - Jordan, Joe wants to know if you have the deed."

Hamilton said, "I had the deed, but its ashes lay in the bottom of my waste basket. We have a small problem. The girl and her boyfriend made copies. They said if anything happens to them, the people they gave the copies to will release it to the press."

Joe wrote back, and Brodsky said, "Jordan you're done; we'll handle it from here. And he says thanks for doing a great job."

Hamilton thought about the irony of Bobby Kennedy having the deed that linked Bobby's father, Joe, to organized crime after Bobby had waged such war against the mafia. Hamilton knew the deed contained information that could not be exposed. The deed transferred Kennedy's ownership of the El Rancho Casino to Frank Costello, a mob person. At least the original deed was destroyed and never recorded. His only concerns were the copies that were made by Val. Perhaps he could still figure out a way to get the money hidden by Virginia, and the copies of the deeds in one more deal.

Chapter 25

The clear sky was bright blue without a cloud in sight. It was a very nice seventy-five degree with just a hint of a breeze. Val and Artimis decided to take a break from all of the ordeals presented in the past few weeks and they went to Disneyland. The crowd was light for this particular Wednesday in May because kids were still in school. Val and Artimis were fortunate not to have to wait in long lines. They were able to get onto most of the "E" ticket rides such as "The Haunted Mansion," "Pirates of the Caribbean," and "The Matterhorn." Val's favorite attraction was "The Hall of Presidents" which was free to enter.

Val and Artimis had just finished a magical day at the park and were exiting through the park's return gate. They planned on returning that evening for the fireworks show. Upon leaving the Magic Kingdom each person stuck out their left hand palm side down as an attendant stamped it.

In order for a person to re-enter the park, each person passed through a special dedicated turnstile and put their left hand under a black lamp. The lamp showed a special mark, allowing them to re-enter.

As they were exiting the park, Val was curious about the ink used to stamp their hands which allowed them to return later that evening. She asked the attendant, "What type of ink is used on the pad?" The attendant struck the pad and then Val's hand.

"I'm not certain," the attendant said. Val did not give the matter much thought as she exited.

On the tram taking them back to the parking lot area, Val discussed with Artimis the possibilities of using black light for special effects in movie productions. Val looked at the back side of her left hand. She could not see the invisible ink used to stamp her hand so they could get back in the park later. She was in deep thought thinking about the black light posters she had seen in various stores. The psychedelic designs that glowed when a black light was shined on them intrigued her. She was jolted back into reality as the tram came to an abrupt stop and the driver announced "Chip and Dale. This lot is for those parked in Chip and Dale." Val and Artimis quietly exited the tram. Although it was only four o'clock, they were both thoroughly exhausted from the day's activities.

Rather than drive an hour each way to return that evening, Artimis suggested they check-in at the Disneyland Hotel, catch a quick nap, and stay overnight. Val agreed.

After their restful sleep, feeling refreshed and regenerated, Val and Artimis made their way back to Disneyland to watch the fireworks show. Standing approximately half-way down Main Street just before the Carnation Ice Cream Shop, they had a perfect view of Sleeping Beauty's Castle.

The crowd grew larger and larger watching for Tinker Bell's flight from the top of the Matterhorn to a tall tree structure behind the Fantasyland Skyway Station. At exactly 9 p.m., the crowd was buzzing in awe as Tinker Bell made her flight to start the fireworks gala. It was a breath-taking experience for all who witnessed the colorful explosions high above the Castle that were set to music.

After the fireworks display, a mosaic extravaganza of exploding color sparkles that lit up the night, Artimis and Val made their way back through the crowd to the Emporium, the largest store inside the Disneyland Park. It offered something for everyone.

The shop was the first one on Main Street itself, on the left side, just behind Town Square. The shop was hidden behind several different facades and had multiple entrances. Entrances were located in Town Square, Main Street U.S.A., and the Liberty Arcade.

The inside of the shop was one big room. The front was where you would find Disney clothing and related items. At the far end of this section, there was a glass cabinct on the wall displaying the newest Disney jewelry. In the middle of the shop were more items such as mugs, drawing items, small toys, key-chains, etc. The walls at the middle of the shop were mostly used to sell themed items, such as the Pirates of the Caribbean.

As Val made her way through the shop, she came across a secluded area in a far corner where posters were sold. Much to her amazement, a few black lights were for sale. Intrigued by the idea of invisible ink and how a black light might be used to enhance the special effects in movie productions, she purchased one of the bulbs. She smiled as she strolled toward the front entrance of the shop where she and Artimis and agreed to meet.

Chapter 26

The mahogany desk shook violently as the sound of Mickey's fist pounding on it reverted throughout the office. "What the hell do you mean?" Mickey Cohen yelled at Michael Caldwell.

"It seems Val and her boyfriend aren't in any hurry to solve the rest of the clues," Caldwell calmly told Mickey. Caldwell continued, "The tail said the two have been at work and just yesterday went to Disneyland. Apparently, since they left Chicago and Jordan backed off they've been lying low."

Mickey's face turned a shade of red Caldwell had never seen before. His veins started to bulge. Before he said another word, Mickey rubbed his chin and sat down in the black leather chair behind his desk.

With his hands folded and resting on the desk, Mickey calmly said, "Okay, if they won't take the initiative to find the loot, we'll give them some incentive."

Caldwell asked, "What do you have in mind?"

Mickey said with a straight face, "Invite them back to Vegas and have them bring everything they have with them on the pretense that I want to help them finish their quest."

Caldwell looked at Mickey quizzically, wondering what he was up to. "Do you think they'll fall for it?"

Mickey shook his head no. "Of course they won't, but they think I have some special knowledge of Virginia. Just get 'em here."

Caldwell said, "You're the boss. I'll personally invite them." He left Mickey's suite without further discussion.

Mickey thought of Caldwell as his attorney and his inside man used to gather information from Thornton. In actuality, Michael Caldwell was now employed by Thornton who asked Caldwell to re-infiltrate Cohen's organization. Thornton remained suspicious of Caldwell because of all of Caldwell's inquiries about Valentina. To be safe, Thornton paid Caldwell handsomely and kept a close eye on his activities.

Vegas was a short airplane flight to Los Angeles. Caldwell caught a flight to L.A. that had made a stop over from Chicago. He arrived at MGM Studios shortly after two pm. As he approached the doorway to Val's office, he wondered if someone was watching him as they had Sam. He entered the door with an ease of familiarity. As he entered the office, he saw Artimis holding a cup of coffee talking with Val.

"Hey Val, Artimis, my name is Michael Caldwell, and I'm an attorney for Mickey Cohen," he said.

Val thought to herself, *not again.*

"What does Mickey want now? Artimis replied.

"Mickey asked for you and Val to visit him this weekend in Vegas. He's picking up the tab for your trip." Val was standing right in front of Caldwell.

"Why?" Val asked.

Caldwell removed his sunglasses, and, with a straight face, said, "He wants to help you finish solving the mystery of Virginia Hill."

Val showed no sign of emotion and with a poker face, asked, "Really?"

Caldwell continued, "Yeah, he says he has some more information that can wrap this thing up. He just needs to see everything you have."

Artimis glanced over in Val's direction and nodded yes.

"Alright, we'll be there," Val said.

Caldwell replied, "Excellent. One more thing, Mickey said your car will be ready, and will be like brand new."

Val smiled and asked Caldwell if he wanted a cup of coffee or soda. Caldwell politely declined and handed Artimis the airline tickets for their weekend flight to Vegas. "We'll have a limo pick you up at the airport," Caldwell said.

Val asked, "Will you be joining us this weekend?"

Caldwell smiled and said, "No, I'm heading to Chicago." Caldwell made his way toward the door to leave. He hesitated as he opened the door, turned toward Val and Artimis, and said, "Have a good weekend. I hope you find what you're looking for." Val and Artimis both noticed the apprehension on Caldwell's face as he left. Both wondered if something ominous was going to happen next. Nothing did.

Chapter 27

Val removed a small white envelope from underneath the carpet in her closet with trepidation. She looked at the key on the gold chain hidden with a peace medallion in the envelope. She decided she could not trust Mickey any further. She put the key back into the envelope and replaced it underneath the carpet.

Twilight was ending as the darkness of the night fell across the west coast. The sky was clear, but the stars could not be seen clearly because of the city's lights. There was only a sliver of moon. Val closed the curtains to the front room and sat down on the soft, leather couch. She spread the items from the envelope she received from Shaw across the coffee table to look at everything one final time before giving them to Mickey Cohen.

She sat examining each photo and each card intensely trying to figure out what the last clue on the Queen of Diamonds meant. Nothing made sense. The Queen of Diamonds was from the Sahara but there were no photos that referred to the Sahara other than the one with Virginia and Chick standing in front of it. All of the other cards were connected somehow to other casinos in Vegas. She repeated the words written on the Queen of Diamonds to herself over and over, "Your journey's end is not where you think. Oh what a tangled web we weave when first we practice to conceive. This ice will frost you without a chill. Finders keepers - - who needs a will. Look not in the obvious place, or else you'll end up with egg on your face." Val thought to herself that the Sahara would be the obvious place to look, yet that was not the place where what she was looking for would be hidden.

Val rubbed her eyes and took a sip of coffee. She knew it was going to be a long night. She looked toward the kitchen and saw the black light's box sitting on the counter. She got up from the couch, opened the box, and removed the bulb. As Val held the bulb in her hand, she had a thought. She brought out a small lamp that sat on her nightstand. She removed the bulb in the lamp and screwed in the black light bulb. She plugged the lamp into a nearby socket and turned it on. She then turned off all of the other lights in the house. Her teeth glowed bright white. All of the dust in the apartment appeared like stars.

Val picked up a photo from the coffee table and examined it. Nothing on the front of the photo appeared. She turned the photo over and was startled to see a message appear. "What the hell," She thought to herself.

There, in front of her eyes, was a message that read, "Mickey is not to be trusted. Thornton is the only person to trust."

She picked up another photo and turned it over. Another message appeared. It read, "5865 Aspen Drive, Bow Mar, Colorado - no one knows." She then picked up another photo. The message on the back read, "Key is to the strong box - I hid it well." Val was giddy with the messages she read on each of the photos. Adding the messages on the back side of each photo along with the clue on the card, she was able to figure out where Virginia had hid something she did not want anyone else to find. She quickly turned on the regular lights, turned off the black light, and put everything away.

Once finished, she called Artimis, "Hey, get over to my place as soon as you can!" she said.

Artimis, half asleep, said, "What now?"

Val did not want to take a chance discussing what she had found on the phone, and said, "I'm horny and want you come over and fuck my brains out."

Artimis realizing that something was up said, "See you in twenty minutes."

Artimis was at Val's place in record time, and in a dry voice said, "What's up?"

Val turned the lights off and turned the black light on, "What do you think?" she asked.

Artimis was in no mood for games, "You called me over at two a.m. in the morning to show me this?" he asked.

Val smiled and said sarcastically, "No silly - I just wanted to see you." Now more seriously she continued, "But the black light showed some hidden messages on the back of each photo. I figured out where we need to go to get what Virginia left for me, and I don't trust Mickey or Jordan Hamilton. It feels like someone is always watching us so we need to keep this information on the down-low."

Artimis' eyes opened wide as he realized what Val just told him. "No shit," he said. "What's your plan?" he asked.

Val said, "First things first - let's get some sleep and tomorrow we'll take the photos to the office and have them professionally reproduced so that Mickey thinks he's getting the originals. We'll also get a key similar to the one that was given to me by Peter Lawford.

We'll play along with Mickey and give him what he wants. While he's trying to figure everything out, you and I will sneak off to where Virginia hid whatever it is she wants me to find."

Artimis said, "Sounds like a plan to me. By the way, where are we going?"

Val was already half-undressed getting ready for bed, "Denver, Colorado."

Artimis got half-undressed himself and climbed into bed next to Val, "Works for me." Within a few minutes, both were fast asleep.

Chapter 28

Friday evening arrived quickly for Val and Artimis, but not soon enough for Val. A limo was waiting at McCarran Airport in Las Vegas to pick them up and take them to the Flamingo. By now, the staff was familiar with the two, and they were treated like royalty.

The bell hop took them to their suite. It was incredible, with a separate living room, hot tub, wet bar and all the amenities of a small lavish apartment. As Artimis tipped the bell hop, he asked if there was anything else they needed. Artimis said, "No, thank you." The bell hop left.

Within five minutes of being in their suite, the phone rang. "Now what?" Val said with a surprised tone in her voice. She picked up the receiver and said, "Hello."

Mickey Cohen was on the other end of the line. "Hello, Val. You and Artimis find your accommodations acceptable?"

Val responded, "Yes, thank you. You're most gracious and generous. These digs are sweet."

Mickey was not wasting time. "Did you bring everything?"

Val responded, "Of course I did."

"Okay, bring it to me. I'll see you and Artimis in my office in ten minutes," he said. With that, Mickey hung up the phone.

Ten minutes later, Artimis and Val arrived at Mickey's office.

"Let's see what you brought," he said before Val and Artimis had a chance to get comfortable. Val walked over to his desk and dumped the contents. "Here it is - - all of it," she said.

Mickey started to sort through the photos, the letter from

Virginia, and the playing cards. He picked up the Queen of Diamonds and read the scribbled message, "Your journey's end is not where you think. Oh what a tangled web we weave when we first practice to conceive. This ice will frost you without a chill. Finders keepers - - who needs a will. Look not in the obvious place, or else you'll end up with egg on your face."

Val watched Mickey intently. "So what does it mean? Your lawyer, Michael Caldwell, said you could help us decipher the message."

Mickey held the card in his left hand, eyeing it as he studied it intently. "I haven't a clue," he said.

Mickey looked at Val and Artimis. His once pleasant facial expression turned to an ice cold glare. Val and Artimis had never seen this side of Mickey before. It was a look that meant business and was not to be taken lightly.

He put the card down and said, "Tell you what, you two leave this with me and give me the weekend to figure it out. In the meantime, have fun and maybe Artimis will give us a chance to get back some of that money he won. What do you say?"

Val smiled, knowing it was useless to turn down Mickey's offer. "Of course we'll leave this with you. Besides, it's better in your possession than ours - it's not worth dying over."

Mickey's expression turned passive, he smiled and said, "Great . . . then it's settled." With that, he escorted Val and Artimis to the door and said, "Have fun. Oh, one more thing. Your Mustang is with the valet. Just call them, and they'll bring it round for you."

Val and Artimis left Mickey's office, thinking they did not stand a chance if Mickey figured out the clues. Worse, if he figured out he had been duped with the duplicate photos.

The weekend went by without incident. Val and Artimis spent most of their time at the pool, shopping, and in their room. They decided it was better not to gamble during this particular trip. Early Sunday morning, they checked out of their suite. They had not heard from Mickey and left without asking him if he had made any progress.

Val knew for sure that he would never figure out the clue on the Queen of Diamonds without knowing the clues on the back side of the photos. The reproduction photos looked exactly like the originals. The boys at MGM had done a spectacular job in duplicating them. Once Val decoded the message, she destroyed the original photos. Even if Mickey could figure out where Virginia had hidden the money he did not have the key to open the box.

Val and Artimis drove the Mustang to a filling station near McCarran airport on the way back to Los Angeles. Once inside the station, a man and woman matching the description of Val and Artimis passed them in the aisle. Val slipped the keys to her Mustang into the hand other woman as they passed each other. Val and Artimis waited to make sure the two look-a-likes got into her car and drove off. After the Mustang exited parking lot, another car pulled out tailing the Mustang.

Artimis and Val waited another fifteen minutes in the station's small store area. Outside, a light green Chevy Impala pulled up front, honked once and waited as Val and Artimis got inside. The car drove off with its passengers.

The driver of the Impala handed Val airline tickets. "Here are the tickets you requested." You're traveling under the names of Mr. and Mrs. John Smith," he said. Artimis watched the driver carefully. Nothing else was said as the car pulled into the airport departure lane.

Val and Artimis exited the vehicle and made a beeline straight for the gate. They were booked on a Delta Airlines flight from Las Vegas to Denver, Colorado. Only one person other than the driver of the Impala knew where they were heading.

Val and Artimis were provided the airline tickets by Nathaniel Thornton. All of the arrangements were booked in alias names using a local travel agency under the law firm's account. Artimis had withdrawn five thousand dollars to pay for their expenses while they were gone. By the time whoever was following the Mustang realized they were tailing the wrong people, Val and Artimis would be long gone.

Back at Val's apartment, the Val and Artimis look-alikes were greeted by two men waiting for their arrival. The two men looked at each other as the imposters asked if they would like a drink. They accepted.

The men from the black sedan looked puzzled when they arrived, knocked, and saw the two other men in the apartment.

"What are you doing here?" they asked.

"Same thing as you, you goof ball. We're under orders to make sure Val and her companion doesn't talk."

The other man said, "Yeah, well, we're here to make sure they stay alive until our boss has what he needs."

The imposters watched as the goons made jerks of each other, pointing fingers and wondering who was going to do what next. The Artimis imposter became tired of the charades and finally spoke up and said, "Mind if we leave? Oh, and lock after you're done here." The imposters smiled. They exited the apartment knowing the stunt went off without a hitch, and also that they were lucky to be alive.

* * *

The air was crisp and smelled of fresh pine as Val and Artimis drove their rental car through a suburb of Denver. It was sixty-eight degrees with clear blue skies. They had rented a metallic blue 1968 Buick Gran Sport Skylark, with tan leather seats and a blue plastic dash. As Artimis drove, Val sat in the passenger seat thinking about what she might find hidden.

Artimis and Val were traveling incognito under the name of John and Lisa Smith. Everywhere they went, they paid cash. They kept a low profile. There was no paper trail to find them.

Val wore a shoulder-length brunette wig and dark sunglasses. All in all, she looked like eighty percent of the other women in society. Nothing distinguished her or made her stand out; she blended in perfectly. Artimis cut his hair into a neat businessman's style - Gone were his long locks of sandy brown hair. He kept his face clean shaven. Everything they owned was with them in the trunk of the car. They knew this was a one-way trip.

Before traveling to Vegas, Val cleaned out her personal belongings from the apartment. She paid a full year of rent upfront for her roommate, Annette, and left five thousand dollars cash in an envelope for her with a note saying goodbye. The note only indicated that she felt her life was endangered and was leaving for her own safety.

Artimis, too, had cleaned out his apartment and paid the landlord to break his lease. The only explanation Artimis gave his landlord was that he took a new job in a different city. The landlord never pressed him for more details. He was only too glad to get paid and to keep the furniture Artimis left behind.

Val called her mother and father from a pay phone. She explained that she and Artimis were leaving Los Angeles permanently, and she would not be able to contact her for a long time. They had a long conversation and many tears were shed. Martha and Stewart understood why their daughter had to disappear.

Both Val and Artimis turned in their resignations to MGM Studios on the Friday they left for Vegas. Val used the story that she accepted a position in Chicago to work for a chemical company. Artimis said he needed time for personal reasons. They each gave two week's notice but were told not to return. Neither took anything from the office so as to give the appearance they were going to return in case anyone was watching. Even their passports were in their alias names of John and Lisa Smith. Nothing was left to chance.

Chapter 29

Mickey Cohen's head felt like an inebriated melon. He had been drinking heavily the night before, frustrated that he couldn't figure out the last message on the Queen of Diamonds. He had studied and examined every photo in great detail. He went so far as to use a high-powered magnifying glass to scrutinize each detail in the photos. But he could not figure out the message. He inspected the key Val gave him, never thinking it was a fake.

Mickey picked up the receiver to the phone and slowly dialed a number. "Jordan, this is Mickey Cohen," he said.

"Any luck deciphering the message?" Jordan asked.

Mickey replied, "None."

Jordan continued, "What do you propose we do?"

"I'm not sure," was Mickey's response.

Jordan kept calm as he discussed with Mickey the fact that Val and Artimis had given both of their teams the slip.

Jordan had had a long discussion with Joseph Kennedy's assistant, Jack Brodsky. Brodsky assured Hamilton that Joe was done with the girl and her friend, and that Hamilton could do what he wanted. Bobby's presidential campaign was running smoothly. He was leading the other candidates in the primary and Joe was confident Bobby would get the party's nomination at the Democratic Convention in Chicago. The original deed was burned and there was no sense in upsetting anyone at this point.

After Jordan updated Mickey of his conversation with Brodsky, Mickey asked, "So Joe is backing out of this for sure?"

Jordan was smug with his reply, "Yep, just you and me to split the loot. According to the last information I had, it should be close to two million dollars."

"What about Meyer Lansky?" Mickey inquired.

Jordan said, "Not to worry. Lansky's got so much fucking money he won't notice. Besides, who's going to tell him? You?"

"Of course not," Mickey replied.

Jordan ended his conversation with Mickey. Shortly afterwards Mickey was greeted in his office by Luigi and Alfonso. "Jordan sent us over to see if we could be of some assistance," Luigi said.

Mickey invited the two men into his office suite. "Be my guest," he said as he offered the men a drink.

As Alfonso and Luigi started to look through the photos, cards, and other items on the desk, Luigi picked up the key. He held it in his right hand and brought it close to his face to get a better look at it. "Hey, what's this?" he asked Mickey as he held the key in his direction.

"That's the key Val was given by Lawford when you two were with her," he said.

Luigi glanced at Alfonso then glared at Mickey. His nostrils flared, and his face turned a bright shade of rosy red. "No, it ain't," he said, keeping a close watch on Mickey.

"What do you mean this isn't the key?" Mickey shot back, his face turning stone cold.

"Just what I said, this ain't the key I saw Lawford give the broad," Luigi said.

Alfonso moved the photos around and picked up the one of

Virginia sitting with Benjamin Siegel, the photo from the envelope Lawford gave Val. "Hey boss, this isn't the original photo."

Luigi took the photo out of Alfonso's hand. He looked at it and said, "You're right. The water ring is missing."

Mickey chimed in, "What water ring?"

Luigi put the photo down and stared at Mickey, "Alfonso here put his glass on this photo when we were with those two. The broad was pissed off at him because the sweat from the glass left a water ring on the photo. This photo is clean - it's missing the watermark."

Mickey sat down in his chair. His head was banging like it was being beaten like a drum. "Damn her," is all he said.

Alfonso and Luigi stood in front of Mickey's desk looking at him with disdain. Luigi pushed everything off of Mickey's desk. Papers with his notes, the photos, the cards and everything else on the desk flew off in all directions. "This stuff is worthless garbage," Luigi yelled out.

Mickey looked at Luigi and then turned toward Alfonso, "You finished? Get the fuck out of my office."

Alfonso pulled a snub-nosed revolver with a silencer out of his vest pocket and shot Mickey twice. The pistol made two thud sounds as the lead slugs hit Mickey in his head as Alfonso said, "With pleasure."

Alfonso and Luigi exited from the office suite as Mickey sat in his chair, his head flung back with blood oozing out.

Chapter 30

The Buick Skylark pulled into the driveway of a secluded area located on Aspen Drive, in Bow Mar, Colorado. It was the only place in the Denver Metro area to experience a quiet country setting with open space and expansive views. The people who lived in Bow Mar cherished their privacy and the small town atmosphere.

The home located on Aspen Drive was a two thousand, two hundred fifty-two square foot, single level home with white vinyl siding. It was well hidden from the main road by several large pine trees. Val rang the doorbell while Artimis waited in the car. No one answered. She went around to the back of the house and peered through the windows. It appeared that the place was deserted.

She looked around first to see if she could find a key. After a few minutes of searching, she then looked under the boulder near the patio and found a door key. She picked up the key and went back to the front door. She placed the key in the lock, turned it to the left, unlocked the door and went inside. She called out several times, "Anybody home? Hello," but the place was vacant.

After a few moments, Val opened the door to the garage. It was completely empty. She then opened the garage door and motioned Artimis to pull in. He parked the car and quickly closed the garage door. They went back into the house to look around.

The inside of the house was sparsely furnished. The kitchen had a small table with four chairs. The family room had a black leather sofa, a wood and glass coffee table, a black and white television set and a few paintings hanging on the walls. The wood floors and area rugs were clean. The living room was empty. The master bedroom had a queen size bed, a dresser with a mirror, and two nightstands. The dresser drawers and night stand drawers were empty. The other bedrooms were completely empty.

The refrigerator was empty but working. Val turned on the lights in the kitchen. They worked, so the electricity was turned on as was the water. Artimis opened a few of the kitchen cupboards. Other than a few dishes and pots and pans, nothing else was in the house. There was no food anywhere. Even the bedroom closets were empty. Despite appearing that the house had been empty for several years, everything was clean, neat and well-maintained. Even the yard was groomed.

The house was left just as it was when Virginia was alive. Nothing was out of place. Val and Artimis began searching through the kitchen drawers and behind pictures hanging on the walls. Neither one of them found anything.

In an act of frustration, Val sat down on the tobacco brown leather sofa. Putting her hand on the sofa, she thought it was odd for this piece of furniture to be in the home. It just did not quite seem to fit with the rest of the decorum. The leather was a soft dark brown with an antique nailhead accent along the edges and on the bottom front of the sofa. Val got up and decided to look in the basement.

She opened the door and Artimis asked, "Where are you going?"

Val responded, "I'm checking out the basement to see what's down there."

Artimis followed Val down the stairs. The basement had a washing machine and dryer for doing laundry and nothing else. It was clean and free of dust.

"Hmmm," Val said as she looked around. In the corner opposite of the washing machine and dryer was a deep freezer. Val opened it cautiously. "Ugh," she cried out as the smell overtook her. The freezer was not plugged in.

Artimis went over to the freezer; put his hand over his mouth and nose, quickly opened the door and looked inside. As quickly as he opened it, he closed it to keep the stench inside. It was empty.

Val had a hunch and motioned to Artimis to help her move the freezer. They each grabbed an end and moved it away from the wall. Under the freezer was a metal plate. Artimis reached down and lifted the plate from its spot. Under the metal plate was a hole that held a metal, fireproof strong box. Artimis tried to lift the strongbox, but it was fastened to the ground. The concrete floor of the basement had been carefully removed for a sunken portion to be put in to hold the strong box. The top of it was approximately twenty- inches by twenty-inches and had a key lock on it.

Val took the rope chain, holding the key, off her neck. She fit the key into the strongbox's lock and turned it to the right. It clicked, and she opened the lid to the strong box.

What looked like a safe deposit box was tightly fit into the strongbox. Val removed the inner box, which measured about twelve inches deep. She opened it as Artimis looked over her shoulder. Inside it contained fifty stacks of one hundred dollar bills about five hundred thousand dollars, an original Trust document entitled "Valentina Benjamin Trust," and certified copies of adoption papers. There was also a note that said, "Go talk to Thornton he has all of the answers." The inner box also contained a deed to the property where the box was hidden. It indicated that the property belonged to the trust in Val's name.

She quickly put everything back into the box, closed it, replaced the metal plate and had Artimis move the freezer to its original position.

Val and Artimis did not say a word to each other as they made their way back upstairs. Once upstairs, Val laughed out loud and gave Artimis a big hug. "Wow!" she exclaimed.

Artimis smiled and hugged Val back. "Now what?" he asked.

Val glanced around the residence, and said, "Let's get out of here for now. We'll drive back to Denver, find a hotel for the night, and figure out our next move. Somehow, we need to get in touch with Thornton without anyone knowing."

As Artimis backed the car out of the garage, Val said, "That was odd."

Artimis asked her, "What was odd?"

Val turned to face him and said, "There should have been diamonds in the box too." Artimis kept his eyes on the driveway as they pulled onto the main road and asked, "What diamonds?"

Val told him that the clue on the Queen of Diamonds along with the other messages written in the invisible ink suggested there were diamonds hidden.

Both Val and Artimis exclaimed at the same moment, "The leather couch!" The Winston Chesterfield leather sofa was a staple in every room requiring refinement and elegance but it looked out of place in this particular residence. "What a tangle web we weave when first we practice to conceive," Val said out loud.

"Why Val, I do believe the sofa was where you were conceived," Artimis said with a smile on his face.

"Ha ha. Very funny," Val quipped back as she punched him in the right arm affectionately. "When we return we need to get a better look at that sofa," Val said.

Artimis nodded, "I'm with you."

Chapter 31

It's a challenge to pack proper clothing for Chicago in the month of May. One day it might be eighty degrees with beautiful skies and the next it can be forty degrees with the wind coming off Lake Michigan cutting through you like a knife. Val used a pay phone at O'Hare Airport to call Thornton. She used the name Lisa Smith when the receptionist asked who was calling. The receptionist put her call right through to Thornton's private line.

"Mr. Thornton, Lisa Smith here. I have a layover at O'Hare for about two hours. Can you meet me at United Airlines Gate 10?" Val asked.

Thornton recognized the name and responded, "Give me thirty minutes plus or minus a few depending on traffic." With that, he hung up the phone and simply told his receptionist he was going to be out for the rest of day. Thornton grabbed his hat and left without saying anything further.

* * *

Jordan Hamilton was sitting at his desk in his lavishly furnished office. Three of his bodyguards were milling around in the lobby area. The man known only as The Mechanic walked into the lobby holding an attaché case in his left hand; after the bodyguards patted him down he was given the go ahead to go on back to Hamilton's office.

He entered the office through an open door. Hamilton looked at The Mechanic as he placed the attaché case on one of the chairs in front of Hamilton's desk. "Can I help you," Hamilton asked suspiciously, eyeing the stranger.

The Mechanic said, "Mickey sends his regards."

Hamilton's eyes widened as his mouth wrenched tightly. "Mickey's dead," Hamilton said.

"I know," said The Mechanic as he pulled a .38 caliber revolver with a silencer from the attaché case. He pointed it at Hamilton, and pulled the trigger three times: pop, pop, pop. The gun made a noise hardly noticeable to anyone in the lobby of the office.

Two bullets entered around the area of Hamilton's heart, the third went into his forehead about an inch above the bridge of his nose.

As quickly as The Mechanic entered the office, he disappeared through a back entrance. Hamilton sat in his leather chair, his eyes wide open, as blood flowed down the front of his nose. Blood oozed from his chest and covered his white shirt. The morning papers only reported that Hamilton was gunned down mob-style.

* * *

Thornton met Val and Artimis at United Airlines, Gate 10. Val still wore her shoulder-length brunette wig and dark sunglasses, blending in with the crowd. For the most part, she was invisible. Artimis also looked non-descriptive, wearing a pair of blue jeans, a tie-died shirt, a baseball cap, and sunglasses.

Thornton sat across from Artimis and Val. He spoke softly, almost in a whisper. "So, where are you two heading now?" he asked.

Artimis leaned forward and said with a smile, "Miami for a few days, then back to Colorado."

Thornton grinned, "Val, your financial affairs are all in order.

The trust which holds your primary assets is protected and as confidential as legally possible. If you need any funds or need to make any changes, call Michael Caldwell. He's the attorney handling your case."

Val looked at Thornton and asked, "Why Caldwell? Wasn't he working for Mickey Cohen?"

Thornton had a smile on his face as he looked directly into Val's eyes. "Yes, he worked for Mickey Cohen. But he also worked for me. I paid Caldwell twice what Mickey paid him to keep tabs on everything. Mickey thought it was his idea for Michael to work for my firm. What Mickey didn't know was Michael Caldwell was already employed by our firm. He is the person that got word about The Mechanic being hired to put a hit on you at MGM. Caldwell persuaded the Mechanic to intentionally miss shooting you. Let's just say he intervened on your behalf. Unfortunately, Caldwell was not aware that Sam was also a target."

Val, feeling a little better about her situation, turned to Artimis and then back to Thornton. "I have one more question that still needs answering," Val said.

"What's your question?" Thornton asked.

Val said, "My mother, Martha, said I had a guardian, that someone was always watching her and my father when I was growing up. That whenever I wanted or needed something, it would always be taken care of. Were you that person?"

Thornton smiled; his eyes shone brightly like a proud parent watching a daughter grow up and move out on her own. He said,

"Sort of. I hired private investigators to keep an eye on your parents and you. They would report back to me if anything appeared to need to be taken care of. If anything needed to be paid for, I would send the funds, and it would be done. Virginia set up a trust in your name. All of your money is in various accounts with E.F. Hutton. I made special arrangements for a check in the amount of ten thousand dollars to be deposited into your checking account each month starting next month. The trust is set up to last at least another fifty years if not more. A word of caution, keep a low profile. No need to let anyone know how much you're worth. It will keep you out of a lot of trouble."

Val looked at Thornton with sad eyes and asked, "Is someone watching the home in Colorado, too?"

Thornton nodded his head "yes" and said, "Yes, for now. We paid a neighbor to keep the yard maintained and to clean the inside once a month."

Val didn't want to say too much about the Colorado residence and asked, "So, how long will the neighbor keep an eye on the home?"

Thornton said, "Until you two start residing there."

An announcement came over the loud speaker that United Airlines Flight 345 bound for Miami was now boarding. Val and Artimis said their good-byes to Thornton. Thornton assured them that they were safe and that he, in fact, was retiring.

Chapter 32

Val and Artimis returned from Miami to the residence in Colorado. After settling in and making themselves comfortable Val looked at the sofa. Ignoring the cushions, Val, on a hunch, took out a pair of pliers from a kitchen drawer and began to pry one of the nailheads off the left arm of the sofa.

Meanwhile, Artimis turned on the television in another room.

"Damn it," she cried out as blood began to flow from her right index finger.

Not giving in, Val successfully removed the antique nailhead from the top of the left arm of the sofa. She looked at it for a moment, turned it, and dropped it onto the floor. Next, she removed several more of the nail heads until she was able to pry the leather from the frame of the arm. The wood frame had a small hole with a black velvet bag inside it. Val pulled the bag from the sofa's arm and opened it. She turned the bag upside-down, dumped the contents into her hand, and saw several beautiful large diamonds dazzling in front her eyes.

"Hey, Artimis," she called out. Val extended her hand towards Artimis showing him the diamonds. "You thinking what I'm thinking?" he asked Val.

"What a tangled web we weave when we practice to conceive. Help me pry some more of these off." She said.

Val and Artimis quickly removed several more of the nail heads from the leather sofa's other arm. They pulled back the leather from the frame and found another bag hidden inside the wood frame. The bag contained more diamonds. As Val and Artimis embraced their new found "treasure." Their momentary exuberance was broken as they heard Walter Cronkite announce that Robert Kennedy had been shot at the Ambassador Hotel in Los Angeles. They both turned and watched, immediately transfixed by the news.

A bit later, after the initial shock of what Val and Artimis had learned from learned from the television subsided, they tore the leather sofa apart inch by inch. Only the frame of the arms contained bags with diamonds inside them. In total there were fifty-two diamonds of various sizes, each being at least one carat in weight.

Val made some inquiries at a local jeweler as to the value of the diamonds. Based on her information the gems were worth between one hundred fifty thousand and two hundred fifty thousand dollars depending on their quality and size. With the stock certificates and the cash that had built up in the trust account, her total net worth, excluding the house in Colorado, was about one point seven five million dollars, enough for her and Artimis to enjoy the rest of their lives in a quiet retirement.

Epilogue

Artimis, sitting on a thirty-seven foot Tartan Yacht in the Caribbean, wearing only khaki shorts and sunglasses, was talking to Val about their crazy adventure and treasure hunt. "Hey Val, you know this would probably make a good movie. We should write about our escapades."

Val, wearing a red bikini and lounging on a deck chair as the yacht rocked back and forth in the crystal clear Caribbean waters anchored just off Saint Martin, said, "Yeah, we could end it with a voice over from Virginia, 'Las Vegas, for some it is a place where dreams do come true. For others, it is a place for their worst nightmares'."

Artimis knew he would spend the rest of his life with Val. He loved her before he knew about her past and her fortune. Artimis leaned over to Val and said, "We're in this for the long haul, baby. I love you."

Val responded, "I love you, too." The two ended their conversation with a long passionate kiss.

Robert Kennedy was dead. Joe was no longer concerned about anything else at this time. Mickey Cohen and Jordan Hamilton were also dead. As far as Val and Artimis knew, no one else should be watching them or knew their whereabouts. Still concerned for their safety, they maintained their alias of Lisa and John Smith.

Agent Atwood was sitting at his desk when a messenger showed up delivering a small package. The box was addressed to Agent Atwood, FBI Building, Wilshire Boulevard, Los Angeles,

California. It was a plain, white box, measuring approximately three inches by five inches and about two inches deep. Atwood opened the box, his curiosity getting the better of him. Inside the box were a small handwritten note and two white folded pieces of paper shaped to make envelopes.

The note read, "Agent Atwood, thank you for your trust. This is a token of my appreciation." Atwood put the note down on his desk and opened one of the folded pieces of paper. Inside were five magnificent diamonds each weighing at least one carat, if not more. Atwood quickly re-folded the envelope and rapidly opened the other folded paper. Inside were five more diamonds, slightly larger than the others. Again, he quickly folded the envelope.

Atwood looked at the box again and examined it carefully. There was no return address. There was nothing to indicate where it was sent from. Atwood smiled, stood up from his desk, put on his suit jacket and took the two folded pieces of paper and carefully placed them inside his jacket pocket.

The FBI and the other law enforcement agencies were not going to waste much of their time or resources trying to solve the killings of Mickey Cohen, Jordan Hamilton or several of the other people killed of late, because they were known members of the crime syndicate. They had been known killers.

Atwood tossed the empty box into the waste basket near his desk. He smiled as he strolled out of the office enjoying the beautiful Los Angeles day, knowing he still had several other crimes to solve.

More
David Medansky!

Please turn the page for a
preview of

Love's
Battlefield

David Medansky's
next novel.

Chapter 1: May 21, 2001.

Bang!!! Judge Susan Roberts slammed down her gavel barking out at the top of her gruff voice, "You're out of order Mr. Caldwell, sit down!" Judge Susan Roberts sat on the bench in her black robe presiding over family law cases in Superior Court of Maricopa County, Arizona. Most family law Judges could only handle being on the Family Law Bench for two years. Judge Roberts had been on the Family Law Bench for more than eight years. At age forty-eight, her long blond hair and hazel green eyes were dull and lifeless. Her youthfulness long gone, she was now a shell of a lady, let alone a person.

Michael J. Caldwell was a good looking, not quite handsome attorney. At age thirty-five, he had a burly build with a muscular tone. Standing six feet tall his blue eyes, sandy brown hair and reassuring smile could calm even his most anxious clients. Yet, he had a demeanor that struck fear into opposing counselors. His ten years of practicing divorce law had diminished his passion for the law and increased his disdain for Judges. Wearing a navy blue suit, powder blue shirt and a wide tie with Donald Duck printed on it he calmly stood delivering his argument before Judge Roberts. The Donald Duck tie was Caldwell statement of how he viewed the judicial system.

Standing, Caldwell spoke knowledgably and gracefully, with an elegance that commanded respect of every Judge before whom he appeared. "Your Honor, this woman has not seen her child in more than three weeks. If you grant the father's request to continue this hearing it will be another three weeks before she can see her daughter. No child should have to go six weeks without seeing a parent."

Judge Roberts glared at Caldwell and the opposing attorney, Frank Rowley. Frank Rowley was a short hefty fellow barely reaching five feet five inches. He weighed two hundred twenty-five pounds as his belly hung over his waist. With dark brown hair and brown eyes, Rowley was a devious, conniving scoundrel that gave attorneys a bad reputation. He was the typical stereotype attorney who was more interested in how much money he could milk from his clients than actually helping them. Rowley could care less about destroying families than doing what was best for his clients or their children. Rowley, wearing a pin stripe dark gray suit, white shirt and solid red tie, was seated at the opposing counsel's table with his client, Mr. Jake Ballard.

Judge Roberts waited for Caldwell to finish his argument and continued, "Counselors, I have had just enough of this – your clients have been fighting over their divorce longer than they were married. I've been sitting here for an hour listening to the two of you bicker back and forth and already I'm exhausted." She glared at the parents, "And the two of you have been doing this since 1996! You people need to grow up and change your behavior cause it's doing serious harm to your child. And Mr. Caldwell, you say another word and I'll hold you in contempt."

Caldwell sat down next to his client, Mrs. Grace Ballard, and glanced at Rowley. Rowley flashed Caldwell a menacing smile which Caldwell simply ignored.

Judge Roberts prolonged the court session rambling off more

of her speech which every divorce attorney had heard ad nauseam. Caldwell showed absolutely no interest in Judge Roberts' words of wisdom. He reached for the pitcher of water sitting on the table in front of him and poured himself a glass.

As Judge Roberts spoke, Caldwell sat in his chair staring into the front of the courtroom thinking to himself, "It's a funny thing about being a lawyer, we work are asses off to get where we're at in our profession, we represent people who hate us and don't want to pay for our services, and yet ninety percent of attorneys would rather be doing something else. Except, of course those attorneys like Rowley that have been identified as minions of Satan."

Finally Judge Roberts ended the hearing and said, "We will continue and finish these proceedings first thing tomorrow morning at eight am. Until then we stand in recess. Mr. Caldwell, Mr. Rowley, I'd like to see both of you in my chambers."

Judge Roberts banged her gavel. The sound reverberated loudly throughout the courtroom and brought Caldwell out of his stupor.

Judge Roberts went back into her chambers and removed her black robe. Under the robe she wore a red blazer, pink button down cotton shirt and a red skirt that rose just below her knees. In every sense she was a professional woman. She sat down in her chair behind her desk lifted the telephone receiver and buzzed her judicial clerk and said, "Send the counselors in please."

The response back from the clerk was, "Yes your honor."

Counselors Rowley and Caldwell each took a seat in chairs in front of Judge Roberts. She started the conversation in a stern authoritative voice, "Gentleman, you two had better put your differences aside or I'll notify the State Bar of what I consider to be unethical conduct on both of your parts. Tomorrow morning I am going to rule in favor of Mr. Caldwell's client and allow the mother to have access with her daughter for the next week. The parents will then alternate one week on and one week off until we go to trial. Mr. Rowley, you'd better make certain that if your client fails to follow my orders he will lose custody of his child. Do I make myself clear?"

Rowley in a low monotone voice and with much deference hiding his shallow and conniving character replied, "Yes, your honor."

Judge Roberts continued, "And you Mr. Caldwell, you'd better instruct your client to make certain she is the ideal mother for the next six months or she'll lose custody of her daughter. I'm telling both of you that if either parent screws up during the next six months I will appoint a guardian ad litem for this four year old girl and send it to juvenile court with the recommendation that both parents lose their parental rights. Now get out of my sight, I have work to do."

With that Rowley and Caldwell both got up from their chairs and left Judge Roberts' chambers. Neither said a word as they left.

At ten o'clock in the morning, Michael Caldwell felt the intense Phoenix sun beating down on him as he left the Courthouse, with his client, to return to his office. The sky was a robin egg blue with a few puffy white clouds hanging overhead. Although the Arizona heat was a dry heat at one hundred and three degrees it was still hot like an oven. Caldwell smiled to himself as he walked with Grace Ballard and discussed Judge Robert's favorable ruling.

Grace Ballard was age thirty-seven, but looked more like age thirty. She wore a dark blue pant suit that offset her bright green eyes. She had her fabulous shoulder length hot toffee colored hair neatly styled in loose wavy curls. Standing at five feet six inches she had a slender build and a muscular tone from working out three times a week.

Grace had been a flight attendant for America West Airlines for twelve years. Because of her passion for traveling she ignored her four year old daughter, Jessica much of the time. Her six year marriage to Jake Ballard was at first blissful, but as the years passed by it became more stormy.

Jake Ballard was a professional insurance agent who had an American Family agency. Jake did very well financially earning more than two hundred thousand dollars per year. He was an excellent father who devoted a lot of time to raising Jessica.

Unfortunately for Jake he retained Frank Rowley to represent him. Rowley had the reputation for being a bull dog unwilling to settle any case. If Jake had hired any other attorney the matter would have been settled years earlier. Instead, it became a nightmare case with false allegations made by both parties and mountains of documents exchanged between the two sides. The only loser in this case was Jessica.

Michael Caldwell drove his 2000 Royal Blue Jaguar S type car into the underground parking garage at the Viad Corporate Center building. The Viad Corporate Center located on Central

Avenue just north of McDowell in Midtown Phoenix, was also referred to as the Viad Tower, and was formerly known as the Dial Tower. The tower was constructed in 1991 for the Dial Corporation and was designed to resemble a Dial soap bar. It was the last major skyscraper to be constructed in Midtown Phoenix.

Michael rode the elevator to his office located on twentieth floor. The elevator door opened and he walked down the hall toward the double doors at the end of the hallway. The reception area of his office suite was lavishly furnished with a coffee brown leather sofa and several matching chairs. There was a coffee table in the middle area covered with several daily newspapers including the Wall Street Journal, New York Times and Arizona Republic along with a few magazines.

Michael walked past several clients, past the receptionist desk toward his office. The receptionist, Jackie Johnson, an extremely attractive young woman was on the phone and didn't have a chance to say anything to Michael before Karen Lewis approached him.

Karen Lewis, age thirty-two, was a gorgeous woman, with a trim figure, soft blue eyes and sunflower short blond hair. Standing five feet four inches she wore blue jeans and a sleeveless pink blouse with ruffles on the front.

Standing next to Karen are her two young boys, John and William, both under the age of ten. Michael raised his hand as if to say, "Wait a minute," as he strolled past her without breaking stride into his office.

Karen gave Michael a quick smile and flashed her perfectly white teeth and moved to sit back down again.

Michael had just removed his suit jacket and sat down in his large office black leather chair behind his mahogany desk as Jackie made her way into his office.

Jackie stood five feet six inches, wore a grey pant suit with a white button down cotton blouse. Her French roast colored hair was pulled back in a pony tail. Jackie was a gorgeous young woman, yet despite her great looks she had a kind and caring demeanor and disposition. Her deep blue eyes sparkled as she looked at Michael and said, "How did it go?"

Michael was in no mood to discuss what took place in Judge Roberts' courtroom and simply said, "Don't ask, stupid judges." Jackie looked at Michael grinned and handed him several messages. She placed a stack of mail on the corner of his desk. As she turned to leave, Michael said to her, "Have Ms. Lewis come-on back." Jackie exited Michael's office without saying another word.

Jackie walked out to the reception area and instructed Karen Lewis to go on back to Mr. Caldwell's office. "Ms. Lewis, would you prefer to leave the boys up front with me? I have some crayons and paper?" Jackie asked.

Karen Lewis replied, "Thank you. Boys stay here with Ms. Johnson and don't cause her any trouble."

Jackie gave each boy a set of crayons and some paper for them to draw on. She then sat back down at her seat and answered the telephone, "Caldwell and Associates, this is Jackie." The voice at the other end asked to speak to Mr. Silverstein, Michael's partner.

"I'm sorry but Mr. Silverstein is in court this morning, would you like his voice mail?" Jackie replied.

The person calling answered in the affirmative and Jackie transferred the call to Silverstein's voice mail.

Michael's office was decorated like any successful mid-level attorney. It had a large law library, a mahogany desk with a large leather chair, two leather chairs for clients to sit in front of his desk, his law diploma and college degrees framed and hanging on the wall as well as a mini bar.

As Karen entered his office, Michael invited Karen to take a seat. Karen sat down in one of the plush client chairs. Michael started the conversation, "What can I do for you Karen? According to my calendar we aren't scheduled to meet until next week."

Karen in a soft, almost sobbing voice said, "I'm sorry Mr. Caldwell, but my asshole ex-husband hasn't paid his child support and alimony for three months and yet he demands to see the kids. He won't stop calling the house. It's practically harassment." Karen continued her rambling and ranting.

Michael looked at her with a blank stare, pretending to be listening, not really caring. He opened the top left drawer of his desk and removed a revolver. He checked the revolver to make certain it had a bullet in the chamber. Karen was oblivious to Michael as he calmly put the gun against his head and pulled the trigger. Bang!!!

Karen yelled at Michael, "So what are you going to do to get some money for me Mr. Caldwell? I'm paying you to represent me."

Michael woke from his day dream. Without missing a beat

he calmly, in a soothing voice said, "Karen, I will file the Petition for Contempt against your ex-husband this afternoon. With any luck we can get a hearing date within the next month. Until then I will contact your ex's attorney and see if he can get him to make a payment. In the meantime you must let him see the kids even if he isn't paying support. I'm sorry Karen I don't make the rules I just have to follow them."

Karen finished venting and felt some gratitude that Michael would be filing a petition to throw her ex in jail. Still, she gave him an unappreciative look as she got up to leave his office.

Michael escorted Karen up front to the reception area. He politely said good bye to Karen and walked back to his office frustrated and disgusted with the entire judicial system.

Michael sat down in his chair and placed both hands upon his forehead trying to relieve the pressure of the morning antics. As Michael sat taking a moment to relax and regain his composure, there was a knock on his office door. Standing in the doorway was Jack Silverstein, Michael's law partner.

Jack Silverstein stood five feet ten inches, had hazel eyes and sandy brown hair parted on the left side. He wore a silk shirt and solid red tie. At age thirty-five, Jack Silverstein looked more like a GQ model than a personal injury and divorce attorney.

Jack held a hard cover book in his left hand with a dust jacket. The title of the book was *When the Witness Came Out*, a sexy legal thriller by Michael Caldwell, author of the almost best-selling *The Judge's Malice*.

Jack said in a mocking tone, "You've reached an all time low with these books haven't you?" Michael retorted in a gruff tone, "I like to write, what you going to do, sue me?"

Jack continued his playful harassment of Michael, "I was hoping you'd aim for something a bit more sophisticated."

Michael played along and replied, "My two newest books are at the publishers right now, and they'll be out in a month."

Jack continued the conversation, "Yeah, what are the titles of these called?"

Michael smiled, "The first is titled *The Day the Juror Died* and I'm not telling you the title of the second. I have two book signings already lined up at the Poisoned Pen.

The Poisoned Pen Bookstore founded in 1989 by Barbara G. Peters was renowned nationally and internationally. It was an independent bookstore that specialized in British mystery and crime fiction featuring hard-boiled cynical characters and bleak sleazy settings, history, and literature of the American Southwest. Located on North Goldwater Boulevard in Old Town Scottsdale's Art District, the store was well known for its heavy schedule of author events such as Clive Cussler and Diana Gabaldon and for Autographed First Editions.

Jack tired of his dialogue with Michael and changed the subject, "You have time for lunch?" he asked.

Michael replied, "Sure."

Jack said, "Great, but first I need to stop back at the courthouse. Judge Graft's clerk called and said I left some exhibits there this morning."

Jack and Michael entered Judge Graft's courtroom quietly.

The courtroom was empty except for the clerk sitting at her desk. The clerk looked up and noticed them as they entered through the double doors of the courtroom. Jack approached the clerk and said, "Thank you," as the clerk handed Jack his exhibits. Without saying another word, Michael and Jack left the courtroom as quietly as they had entered.

Chapter 2

Durant's Restaurant located on Central Avenue was a favorite place for attorneys and politicians to dine during the lunch hour. Durant's was a Phoenix icon that opened in 1950. It's had an inimitable history. The stories might or might not be exactly true. The only certainty was that many celebrities dined at Durant's and countless decisions about the City of Phoenix and the State of Arizona were unquestionably made over one of Durant's porterhouse steaks or prime rib, a glass of bourbon, and a fine cigar.

Durant's didn't look exceedingly notable from the outside, but once inside the pink Phoenix landmark its unassuming exterior was all but forgotten. Most patrons entered Durant's through the kitchen in the parking lot in the rear of the building. Once through the kitchen and inside, the décor was red flocked wallpaper, red leather booths, and dark cherry wood furniture. The servers all wore tuxedos.

Jack and Michael were warmly greeted by the host and immediately seated in a corner booth where they had some privacy.

Although many businessmen enjoyed a martini with their meal, Jack and Michael each ordered a glass of the house Merlot. The server brought a basket of bread along with herbs in garlic oil. Michael ordered a small petite filet while Jack ordered the prime rib. Durant's was renowned for its tender lean and tasty meats.

Michael looked despondent as he spoke, "What's the point of being an attorney anymore? Our clients want us to fight their battles but they don't want to pay us for our time or services. Most of them could give a rat's ass about us. If I dropped dead tomorrow they would step over my carcass on the way to the next attorney's office. I didn't marry their spouse and I certainly didn't sleep with them to have kids, yet they act as if it's my fault for their problems."

Jack interrupted with a broad grin and said, "Oh you mean my office?"

Michael ignored Jack's wistful comment and continued his rant, "Seriously, I'm really tired of this work Jack. I'm fed up with my client's emotional constipation. Is it really my fault that child support payments are late, or that visitation schedules aren't followed, or one or the other spouses was hiding money from the other?"

Jack looked at Michael, took a sip of wine and said, "Emotional constipation, I like that. I'm gonna use that. So why did you become a lawyer Mike?" Jack asked.

Michael replied, "Because of my pop?"

"What about him?" Jack countered. Michael swirled the wine in his glass and as he watched the purplish red liquid move around the glass in a circle said, "He was an attorney. He made it seem like an ideal job until I learned what he really did."

"What was that?" Jack asked.

Michael in a nonchalant voice answered, "Conciliatory to the Montoya crime family."

Jack was surprised and said, "No shit?" Michael lamented, "Yap, I went to Penn State for law school and my dad went to the state pen. He spent twelve years in prison before he committed suicide. Poor bastard!" The conversation abruptly ended as the server brought them their food.

225

The two men quietly enjoyed their meals with little conversation. At the end of their meal they headed back to the firms' office in Michaels' Jaguar. With a 210 horsepower 4.0L AJ-V8 engine, it was powerful, but not really fast. Michael's Jaguar had a royal blue exterior with tan leather seats and faux wood dash. Other than it being a Jaguar there was really nothing distinguishable about the vehicle.

Back at the office Jack was seated in a chair for clients in front of Michael's desk, "I'm worried about you my friend," he said in a serious tone as he looked directly at Michael. Michael responded, "Do you think judges' are wearing pants under their robes?" Jack laughed loudly, got up from the chair and said, "You have a sick mind Mike. I've got work to do. I'll see you later." Jack left Michael's office still laughing to himself.

Michael quickly dictated the petition for contempt for Karen Lewis' case. He placed the tape in his secretary's in-box and went back into his office.

Michael and Jack used one secretary, Audrey Sanderson. Audrey was fortyish, with chestnut brown shoulder length hair with grayish highlights. Her black rimmed glasses hid her dazzling green eyes. She wore a striking Karl Lagerfeld pleated emerald green skirt with a light green pastel blouse.

Audrey was a no nonsense professional legal secretary that commanded everyone's respect and admiration at the firm. Michael and Jack were fortunate to have her as their legal secretary because of her speed and efficiency to turn out pleadings and other legal documents. Audrey was extremely well paid for her position and earned more than most of the attorneys in the Phoenix metropolitan area. Jack and Michael knew she was worth every penny.

Michael sat back in his chair and closed his eyes. He flashed back to a scene that happened in his office just a few days earlier. At a settlement conference with an opposing counsel the clients got into a heated argument. The husband was yelling at Michael's client, "Are you deaf? That silverware is mine! My forks, my knives, my spoons!"

The wife had a shrill voice and yelled back at the husband, "I chose them at the registry, I'm keeping them! You can eat with your fingers for all I care . . . and you're the worst fuck I ever had!"

Fortunately for Michael, the opposing counsel was more interested in settling the matter than having the two clients bicker with each other. They took a break.

Michael recalled his conversation with his client once he calmed her down, "Well Sarah, when would you use the silverware you are fighting over?" he asked. Sarah replied, "Probably at holidays and special occasions." Michael continued, "And when you used the silverware would you remember your ex?"

Sarah quizzically answered, "Probably."

Michael said, "Well, do you want to remember him after your divorced?"

Sarah starting to catch Michael's drift said, "No, not really."

"Michael pushed further, "If your ex had the silverware, when do you think he would use it?"

Sarah answered, "On holidays and special occasions." Michael continued, "And do you think he will think of you when he's using the silverware?"

"Probably," Sarah replied with a slight smile on her face.

Michael asked, "So can he have the silverware?" To which Sarah emphatically said "Yes."

With that Michael and opposing counsel were able to settle the case. Both lawyers were glad to be done with the two whiny, argumentative, and combative clients.

Michael was startled from his day dream when Jackie entered his office and wrapped on his desk to wake him.

Jackie handed Michael an airline ticket, "Michael, here is your plane ticket for Vegas tomorrow. Your plane leaves at eight am." Michael took the ticket from Jackie, "Vegas, oh yeah, thanks Jackie, I don't know what I do without you."

Jackie in a playful, teasing voice smiled and said, "You wouldn't nearly have as much great sex." Michael caught off guard by Jackie's comment, shamefacedly said, "Uh, yeah . . . good point. We'll talk about that later." Jackie smirked turned and left Michael to his thoughts.

Jack waiting in the doorway overheard Michael and Jackie's exchange. Jackie smiled a wicked smile at Jack as she exited the door. Jack looked at Michael as he entered the office, "Mike, you banging our receptionist?"

Michael more alert quipped back, "I'm a lawyer; I'll screw anyone."

Jack, always quick witted, responded, "Lucky bastard. Here are my notes for a new client coming in next week I think you should handle." Michael took the notes and placed them on the credenza behind his desk. Jack noticed the airline ticket on Michael's desk, "Where are you flying off too?"

Michael grinned; his teeth started to show as his grin became a wide smile and beamed, "Vegas."

Jack just shook his head back and forth and walked out of Michael's office without saying another word.

Made in the USA
Coppell, TX
29 December 2019